GOODMANS OF GLASSFORD STREET

MARGARET THOMSON
DAVIS

GOODMANS OF GLASSFORD STREET

B & W PUBLISHING

First published 2007
by Black & White Publishing Ltd
99 Giles Street, Edinburgh EH6 6BZ

1 3 5 7 9 10 8 6 4 2 07 08 09 10 11

ISBN 13: 978 1 84502 164 1
ISBN 10: 1 84502 164 9

Typeset by RefineCatch Limited, Bungay, Suffolk

Printed and bound by MPG Books Ltd

ACKNOWLEDGEMENTS

I am very grateful to everyone who helped me with the research for this book.

Tommy Freeland was once manager of Birrs of Partick and he gave me invaluable information on how a family department store was run. Margaret Burkhill spent twenty years working as a store detective and she told me fascinating stories of her work experiences. Tommy and Margaret spent many hours talking on to my tape recorder and I thank them for their generous help.

Many thanks also to Margaret Lumsden, who told me of her experiences working in Goldbergs and what excellent employers she thought they were.

Ian Sword runs The Granary in Glassford Street and was most helpful.

Then, for the scenes in the Scottish Parliament, I owe a debt of gratitude to Green Party's Chris Ballance, who was most kind and helpful in showing me around. Diane Barr was also very generous in the help she gave me. My sincere thanks to them both.

I am grateful to Adam McNaughton for permission to reproduce the words of his creation, 'The Jeely Piece Song'.

My sincere thanks to my grandson, Martin Baillie, who was

extremely generous in the time he spent with me explaining some of the beliefs and views of the Scottish National Party.

My son, Kenneth Baillie Davis, as always, has been a great help and support, especially with the karate scenes in the book.

I dedicate this book to my dear friends Ann Maclaren and Sharon Mail in appreciation of all their great kindness to me.

I

Wowee-ee, Horatio! There he was, in *CSI: Miami*, tall and slender, his jacket open, one hand hooked in his belt, the other peeling off his shades. He hadn't a conventionally handsome face and she'd never liked men with ginger hair. But Horatio had charisma. His face was creased with caring and she needed caring right now. His eyes narrowed with intense tenderness. And she needed that too. He would lean slightly forward, his head a little to one side, accentuating his caring concentration. But, when necessary, he could suddenly pull out a gun and be determined and ruthless.

She needed that ruthlessness too. She could do without the gun. Though there were times, especially recently, that she felt like killing her son-in-law. Douglas Benson was trying to oust her from her beloved department store, Goodmans of Glassford Street, which had belonged to her late husband. They'd run it together for a lifetime, a happy lifetime. Now that he was gone and she was in her late fifties, Douglas wanted her to retire and give over the business to her daughter, Minna. Of course, that would mean handing it on a plate to him. Poor Minna adored Douglas and was completely under his thumb.

But not Abigail Goodman. Douglas Benson was finding that she was not a soft mark like her daughter. If she ever gave the business over to anyone, it would be to her son, John. At the moment, however, he didn't want the place. John was a Member of the Scottish Parliament and a fervent Scottish Nationalist. He had a flat in the Royal Mile and only visited Glasgow very occasionally to see her. More often than not, she went through to Edinburgh to see him.

John couldn't stand Douglas Benson, and was encouraging her to hang on in there and keep the family business going, and in the same so-called old-fashioned way.

'That's the special charm of it, Mum,' he'd say. 'It's a Scottish family store where the staff are well looked after and they in turn look after the customers. That's why it's still doing so well. Customers nowadays seldom get such personal and caring attention. It typifies all that's good and valuable in Scottish culture – something that Douglas Benson will never understand.'

No, Douglas Benson wanted to change everything inside and out. He wanted to gut the store and completely modernise it. That meant doing away with counters and cutting down on the staff, apparently. He wanted to deal more with England too, buy stores there and God knew where else. He was like a thorn in her side. Continually irritating her. Goodmans of Glassford Street had been running successfully since it first opened its doors way back before the Second World War. Her husband, Tom, had taken over from his father. She had worked in the haberdashery department then. She had come to Tom's particular attention when she'd dressed the haberdashery window one day when one of the window dressers was off sick.

She had been enjoying doing something different and artistic with packets of insoles, safety pins and coat hangers. She hadn't noticed that a little crowd of people had gathered outside to watch her unusual efforts. Tom had been arriving for work and had seen them. Afterwards, he'd summoned her to his office and asked her if she'd like to be a window dresser. She told him honestly that she'd never thought about it because she enjoyed working at the haberdashery counter. She was proud, for instance, that when serving reels of thread, she could immediately select an exact match for any coloured cloth a customer showed her.

Nevertheless, Tom had persuaded her to give the window dressing a try. There were the in-store displays too, and Joyce, the head window dresser, was getting on in years and could do with a bit more help.

She'd helped Joyce for a while and Tom often stopped to admire and comment on her work. Eventually he asked her out and within a year they'd been married.

After she'd had Minna and John, she couldn't settle in the house. There was a very capable nanny to see to their every need. She had become just an entertainer for the children. She'd tell them stories and do puppet shows and make them laugh. Then when the nanny left and the children started nursery school, she decided to go back to work – part-time at first, and then, once the children were older and settled in regular school, she began working full-time. During the part-time period, she made sure she gained experience in all the departments, from the boys' department and the hosiery department, to millinery. She'd even worked in the carpet department for a while.

Once she was full-time, she was helping Tom to run the whole store. She was his partner in every sense of the word. She still missed him. She missed his companionship, missed the business talks and plans they had. Not for expanding, or purchasing other stores. They had several departments in Goodmans on four floors. The basement was used by the workmen and joiners and so on, and for storage. Goodmans sold everything from needles to double beds, but they were always planning to improve the premises and the stock and the conditions for the staff. Like Marks & Spencer's, their philosophy had been that their staff was their greatest asset.

Like Marks & Spencer's too, they provided every facility and help for the staff. An excellent canteen, a hairdresser and a chiropodist.

She, often Tom as well, regularly visited the staff facilities – the canteen, the cloakroom, even the lavatories, all of which were on the fourth floor. As bosses, they had a private lavatory outside their office, but if they found on inspection that the staff facilities were not up to their standards, they immediately ordered improvements.

Douglas Benson wanted to do away with all that. But she was not going to let him. Now he was trying to make out that she was senile, losing the place, incapable. She was not going to let him get away with that either. There were times now, though, that she needed the comfort and reassurance that Tom used to give her. She saw in Horatio's eyes what she used to see in Tom's. Oh, how she missed him. For sex too. He had been a sexually active man right to the end. Horatio awakened these feelings in her every time she saw him on *CSI: Miami*. What would Douglas Benson think of that, eh? He'd be more convinced than ever that she'd gone ga-ga – completely lost the plot.

One of these days, she might write to David Caruso, who acted the part of Horatio so well, and tell him how important he was in her life, how she never missed one of his performances. So far, she'd never even confessed this to John. Nor had she told him about how Douglas was trying to make out that she was becoming more than just old and forgetful. She was losing her mind. He didn't come right out and accuse her of going mad, of course, but that was what he was hinting at. She didn't want to cause more bad feeling than there already was in the family. John would be furious if he knew.

Not long ago, he'd had to be held back from physically attacking Douglas when Douglas had sneered that the Scottish National Party wasn't a political party at all, and Scotland wasn't even entitled to be called a country. It was all 'up in the air' – nothing but mountains and a strip of land. And if they ever reviewed a Scottish fleet, it would only amount to a couple of rowing boats.

Talk about her wanting to kill Douglas? John would have killed him if he hadn't been held back until he calmed down. As he said, it might have been different if Douglas had been English, or of any other nationality, but for a Scotsman to be so disloyal to his own country was absolutely despicable.

Douglas just flung John an impatient look before swaggering away. He wasn't tall like John. He was stockily built and muscular, thanks to his regular workouts in the gym.

'Scotland's constantly being put down,' John said. 'Scotland can't make it alone, Scotland's too poor, too stupid, etcetera. The danger is that people will begin to believe it's true. Whereas we could be like other small European countries – full of confidence and with a belief in what we can achieve ourselves. That's something that independence would give Scotland.'

Confidence and enthusiasm brimmed from every bone of John's tall body and from every hair on his tousled head. She was very proud of him. She didn't go along with everything he said, of course – about the architecture of the Scottish Parliament, for instance. When John's lean face lit up with enthusiasm and his eyes widened and his voice became breathless with eagerness, she never had the heart to tell him she thought the Scottish Parliament looked a monstrosity, especially from the outside. She preferred more traditional architecture. If the Parliament had been situated up on the hill on its own, it would have looked far better, more striking. John admitted that what he would have preferred, and in fact fought for, was putting it up on Calton Hill, but he and the Scottish National Party had been defeated. Building the Parliament crushed in beside beautiful old buildings on the Royal Mile had been a mistake, they both agreed.

She usually smiled and nodded and went along with everything John said. She remembered what an enthusiastic and excitable child he'd been. Nowadays she worried in case other MSPs might be nasty to him and speak to him as Douglas often did. But to give John his due, although he was provocative and often stirred up lively debates, he never lost his temper in Parliament. At least, not in any debates she'd heard, and she'd sat in the gallery of the debating chamber and listened to quite a few.

Douglas and Minna's latest ploy was to keep asking her if she'd babysit her grandchildren, Emily and three-year-old twins, Ann and Garry. Not only babysit in the evening but during the day – especially during the day when she was busy attending to business mail or inspecting new stock. They couldn't get their nanny to put in all the hours necessary, they said. She was sure they were lying and they purposely engineered it so that they could say that the children needed her. They knew she would find it difficult to refuse the children anything.

The children loved her and enjoyed having her look after them, just as she enjoyed being with them. But she believed the nanny was purposely given time off so that she would have to leave what she was doing in the shop and go to the luxury penthouse in George Square.

It wasn't that she didn't enjoy these visits. She did. She sang and recited all the often daft things she remembered her father singing and reciting to her. As often as not, she had the children giggling or squealing with laughter, or trying to copy her and enthusiastically singing with her.

Emily, who was four, had learned quite a few songs and recitations and could proudly repeat them to her mother and father. Like the one that Tom used to sing:

I've got sixpence, jolly, jolly sixpence
To last me all my life.

I've got tuppence to spend,
And tuppence to lend,
And tuppence to send home to my wife.

Minna and Douglas became all smarmy and praised not only Emily but her too, and they told her how she should spend more time with the children.

Even the ones involving drink and drunks that the children belted out were effusively praised.

No friends have I to receive me,
No pretty little wife to deceive me,
I'm as happy as a king, believe me,
As I go rolling home.
Rolling home blind drunk,
Rolling home blind drunk,
By the light of the silvery moooo-ooon.
Happy is the day,
When an airman gets his pay,
Rolling, rolling, rolling, rolling home, blind drunk!

It was good to see the children so happy and having such fun. It was tempting to be with them all the time, every day. But she was not going to let Douglas Benson take Goodmans from her and ruin everything she and Tom had built up.

She refused the last request to go and look after the children in the morning. 'I'm working and I can't take time off during the day any more than you or Minna can. In fact, if the children really need someone, it should be their mother who goes.'

'Minna is needed in the store,' Douglas insisted.

Ignoring him, Abi said calmly to Minna, 'Take the morning off if you need to, dear.'

Douglas's eyes acquired a steely glimmer and, for the first time, Abi knew for certain that he hated her. She felt a stab of fear but immediately quelled it. She was sorry for Minna. She loved her daughter but could have shaken her at times when the poor girl stood looking so miserable and anxious, not wanting to upset her mother but totally incapable of saying a word to Douglas on her mother's behalf. She looked so plain too, with her hair pinned back in a small bun and wearing no make-up.

John once said, 'Minna looks older than you, Mum.'

Certainly, Abi had always tried to look smart. She wore make-up and visited the hairdresser's every week. A little grey was beginning to show and she had it regularly tinted away.

At the last minute, the nanny could work the necessary hours after all, which confirmed Abi's suspicions. She went into the shop at the usual time, feeling slightly sad at first at missing another opportunity of seeing the children. The manager, Mr McKay, had already opened the doors. He always came in early to let the cleaners in and then the rest of the staff. All the staff came in by a special door so that they could be checked. Mr McKay was a keen man with a marvellous memory. He knew by name every employee, male or female, from the cleaners to the store detective. In Goodmans, everyone was called Miss or Mr or Mrs, and whatever their second name was – never by their first name.

Abi savoured the sights and sounds and smells of the place as she moved between the counters. The boys' department, the glassware, the jewellery, the shoes, ladies' underwear, the hosiery, the haberdashery. There was the dry sensation of dust in the wake of the cleaners and a mixture of floor disinfectant and counter polish. The perfumery department enfolded her in delicious aromas of Chanel and Armani. The jewellery department sparkled and twinkled as the staff there arranged their stock in glass cases and fixtures.

Abi said good morning to everyone as she passed, including the cleaner who was washing the stairs.

'Watch your feet, Mrs Goodman.' The woman moved aside to let Abi pass. 'It's still wet. Safer to hang on to the banister.'

'Yes, I will, Mrs Andrews. Thank you.'

She always climbed the stairs instead of taking the lift. Good exercise, she told herself. It was so important to keep fit and well.

Upstairs, there was the children's department. Upstairs again were curtains – there were long solid counters in front of fixtures holding the stock and large tables with stock on them. There were sloping counters with a ledge at the bottom that held rolls of material.

Abi made for the other part of the stairway and climbed up yet again to the third floor, breathing in the musty smell of the carpet department when she reached it. On the third floor was a huge toy department. It had become quite famous. All children, but especially Emily and the twins, absolutely loved the place. There was an exceptionally good buyer in charge there, a Mr Webster, who would trawl to the other side of the globe if necessary, to find and buy the latest and most intriguing new toy.

Up again to the fourth floor where the offices, canteen and other facilities were situated. Her office, which she had shared with Tom, was of huge proportions, with tall windows looking out on to Glassford Street. Tom's desk was still there at the other side of the room from hers. She liked to look over from her desk and see it, and imagine that Tom had just gone out to inspect one of the departments, or speak to the managers or a buyer, and he'd soon be back. Suddenly she experienced one of her little panic attacks. She felt unsafe without Tom. Sometimes she even wondered if Douglas Benson was right and she was going out of her mind. She had become forgetful at times. Names, for instance, were a problem. Often she couldn't remember someone's name, often someone she had known for years. There were times when she had just to say

'Good morning' to a staff member, instead of 'Good morning, Miss Brown' or whatever. Of course, there were a great many people on the staff. It was surely understandable not to be able to remember them all. But she used to remember them all. She had a horror now of forgetting the managers' names or one of the buyers at the daily meetings they held in her office. Douglas and Minna were usually there too.

'There's nothing wrong with me,' she kept telling herself firmly. 'Nothing at all.'

2

After unlocking the big front doors, the next thing Norman McKay did at eight o'clock sharp each morning was switch off the burglar alarm. The lights were then turned on, and then he let the cleaners in. He had been at the shop from just before eight. It was always a strange atmosphere at that early hour – empty, quiet, ghost-like. He found it depressing, especially now that he was so worried about his wife. The cleaners trooped in, then disappeared upstairs to hang up their coats and collect their buckets and mops and other equipment. The lift clanged. Then there was silence again. He was left gazing bleakly at the vast expanse of counters and glass cabinets. He turned to peer into the blackness of Glassford Street. Soon he heard the sharp tattoo of the store detective's high heels.

'Good morning, Mr McKay.'

He looked over his spectacles at her.

'Good morning, Miss Eden.'

Miss Eden was a woman in her forties – a neat, attractive brunette when she arrived, but she could change her appearance very quickly into a shabby woman in a padded coat, headscarf and flat-heeled shoes. She disguised herself as an elderly woman by wearing spectacles and a smooth white wig pinned back in a bun. Or as a housewife clutching a purse and shopping bag. Or someone in a denim skirt and coloured shades. She could be all four on the same day. And if it rained during the day, she put on a raincoat and went out for a few minutes to get the coat wet so that she could blend in more believably with the customers. It was arranged that she came in at different hours each day but always reported to Mr McKay in his office if her arrival was later in the day.

There was a security guard in uniform as well. He mostly just stood at the door, or hovered somewhere nearby. Miss Eden went all over the place. She saved the store a lot of money. By Scots law, two people had to stop the suspected thief, and it had to be outside the shop, so the security guard always helped Miss Eden with that.

The staff began to arrive and Mr McKay wished them all a polite good morning. Then he greeted Mrs Goodman, who was always early, a very conscientious woman. Long may she last, he thought. He didn't trust Douglas Benson. Jobs would be at risk, he felt sure, if Mrs Goodman gave up and Benson took over. But Mrs Goodman looked fit and well, thank goodness. She was a shapely, pretty woman with blonde hair, obviously dyed to hide her grey, but why not? His wife still struggled to look her best despite her debilitating illness. The hairdresser came to the house now to 'touch up my roots as well as give me a nice shampoo and set', as she always said. Dear Jenny. Always being cheerful. If only he could do more to help her.

Determinedly he swallowed over his distress, adjusted his spectacles, and concentrated on the next arrivals. After a time, Mr and Mrs Benson entered. He gave them the usual polite good morning. Benson nodded briefly and without interest. Mrs Benson gave a shy, nervous smile before lowering her eyes and hurrying after her husband. What a frightened little mouse she was. Not a bit like her mother. Or her brother, for that matter. He'd met John Goodman a few times when he'd called to see his mother and take her out for lunch. These were on his occasional free days from his Scottish Parliament duties. He was a really cheery, sparky type and an ardent Scottish Nationalist. Not a bit snobby either. He was always ready for a chat. Usually taking the opportunity to remind everyone to vote SNP, of course. But it was usually just a brief, throwaway cheery line before he left. Nothing prolonged or heavy. Everybody liked John Goodman.

He went round all the departments, checking that every department was adequately staffed and no one was off. Sometimes it meant drafting someone in from another department. Thankfully, he discovered everything was all right. He would have to repeat the procedure when the part-time staff came in. For the present, the staff were all accounted for and busy tidying, replenishing the fixtures, and dusting. Everything that nobody had had time to see to the previous night.

Quite often, because he was the keyholder, he could be called out in the middle of the night. He never knew what was going to happen. It could be a broken window or a fire, perhaps. The police were always in attendance when he arrived at the shop in response to a phone call, and if it was a theft or a burglary, the police went in first. Or at least they always had a dog with them and they sent the dog in first. Not thinking, he often stepped forward to open the door with his key and go in himself. He obviously did not realise what might have happened if he'd walked in then, they told him. He didn't mind so much getting wakened in the middle of the night, but it did upset him to have Jenny disturbed or worried. If only they could have a nurse or maid or full-time carer who would live in. Or, even better, private medical treatment. He'd heard about a new drug that, if not a cure for Jenny's type of cancer, certainly would stop it getting any worse and eventually killing her. It had even been claimed that it was a 'miracle drug' and could indeed cure the illness. But the treatment was only available in a special private nursing home and the cost was horrendous. He simply could not raise that amount of money. It was a big enough worry employing a daily carer, plus a cleaner. The carer had to be with Jenny every minute of every day. The cleaner cleaned the house and did the washing and shopping. He had tried to do more of the housework and shopping himself at first, the housework in the evenings and the shopping in his lunch hour, but it was too much. Anyway, Jenny liked him to sit with her.

'I don't see you all day,' she pleaded. 'I need to treasure every minute of your company while I can.'

There was an ominous ring in her voice that told him she knew she was dying and they didn't have much time left together. He denied it, of course. Both to her and to himself. In his heart of hearts, though, he knew it was true. She was going to die – unless he could find the money to pay for this new private treatment.

A quick glance at his watch told him it was time to go upstairs to the usual morning meeting in Mrs Goodman's office. It had become quite a tense affair, with Mrs Goodman in charge and talking with authority to the buyers and assistant managers, while for the most part Douglas Benson either openly disagreed with her or seethed in silence. The Bensons could have shared the big office with Mrs Goodman but she insisted that they remain based in their own smaller office room next door. He suspected that she was still clinging to the memory of her husband, and a fine man he was. No doubt she couldn't bear anyone to sit in his large, ornately carved chair. No one else attempted to. Rows of ordinary chairs were brought in and lined up. Everyone in front of Mrs Goodman, the Bensons one on each side of her.

This morning several of the buyers were not there. They travelled around a lot. Sometimes they bought stock from warehouses in Glasgow or elsewhere in Scotland, but as often as not, they went down to Manchester or Leeds or Nottingham or London to buy from the big wholesalers and manufacturers there. Mr Webster, the buyer for toys, often went down to South Castle-on-Sea.

It was a lengthy meeting, with Douglas Benson getting his oar in as often as he could. Norman prayed that Mrs Goodman wouldn't forget anyone's name. It was something anybody could do, but it was obvious Benson looked triumphant when Mrs Goodman had a wee lapse of memory. He was trying to prove she was incapable. One of the main ideas he kept arguing for at every meeting was doing away with most of the counters and having stock, especially fashion, hanging on display for customers to rifle through and examine and take into the fitting rooms to try on. Then the customers could take the goods over to one central counter where they could pay. This, he pointed out, was done in every other department store now. True, but as Mrs Goodman said, they were not just another department store. They were different. They were special. They were Goodmans of Glassford Street and people came from all over, not just the city of Glasgow but further afield, to visit and purchase goods.

But look at the money they could save, Benson argued. Yes, indeed, Norman thought. Most of the staff would be ruthlessly cut out for a start. Mrs Goodman reminded him that they were all right as they were. And there was no denying that Goodmans of Glassford Street was not only famous, it was a very profitable business.

After the meeting, Norman went along the corridor to the staff canteen for a cup of tea, before returning downstairs. On the way down, he phoned home on his mobile to check on how Jenny was. He was in the habit of phoning several times a day to ask the carer how his wife was. Sometimes, if Jenny was well enough and was not asleep, the carer would put her on the phone and she'd be able to answer his worried queries. Mostly, however, she was so sedated with painkillers, she was unable to talk to him. Sometimes, when he was at home with her, she'd open her eyes and look lovingly, gratefully at him and she'd manage a smile.

He couldn't bear the thought of losing her. Distress was mounting in him so much that he could barely speak to the chargehands of certain departments he'd purposely come down to see.

The whole day was like that, a continuous struggle to carry on normally and control his fears about losing Jenny. It was a relief when at last it was time for him to make his first journey along to the bank. Some of the takings he carried in leather packets and satchels in a case to put into the bank deposit box. Several journeys had to be made and several different routes taken, and all at different times each day. This was on the advice of the police, who said that thieves soon found out if a regular time was used and so they knew when to attack. After that the times and routes were varied.

There was still plenty of money left in the counting house, of course, to cover the floats he took down to each department every morning to be used as change for any customers who paid cash. Nowadays, though, so much was done either by cheque or plastic card.

He already had an overdraft at his bank. He had a good salary. Nevertheless, it was a constant struggle to cover all the expenses he had. Every night he prayed for some miracle to happen that might make it possible for him to get Jenny into the special nursing home where she would be given the drug that would save her life.

He prayed now as he walked blindly along Glassford Street.

3

Abi went along to The Granary for lunch as often as she could. It was a healthfood shop with a few tables dotted around and high stools at the window shelf. She especially liked their home-made soup and macaroni cheese. But they had a variety of other healthy and tasty dishes she could choose from, as well as sandwiches and cakes. She bought vitamins there too, and calcium tablets and an iron tonic and dear knows all what, in her efforts to remain strong and healthy.

Ian, the owner's son, served in the shop along with two or three pretty young girls. Ian was a tall, nice-looking young man, and always smiling, friendly and helpful. He was there when she arrived and greeted her with his usual cheery smile and 'Hello, Mrs Goodman. It's lentil or tomato soup today, and we've your favourite – macaroni cheese, freshly made just before you came in.'

She ordered the lentil and made herself comfortable at one of the small tables. She never went to the staff canteen at Goodmans in case it made the staff uncomfortable and unable to relax on their lunch break. Douglas and Minna usually went to the restaurant at the Italian Centre. More than once, she'd tried to persuade Minna to have lunch somewhere with her but Minna just became agitated and said that Douglas didn't like going for lunch on his own. She didn't know where all the buyers went to eat. Often she felt sorry for their wives. Buyers were away from home, travelling about on business so much. The manager – for a panicky moment she forgot his name. Then it came back to her, thankfully – Mr McKay, used the staff canteen. She was very fortunate to have such a conscientious manager. Most of the staff were good, conscientious workers. Only occasionally was it found that someone was letting the side down. If it was dishonesty, usually another member of staff would give Miss Eden a hint. Then Miss Eden would watch them and eventually catch them, and they would be dismissed. Miss Eden was exceptionally clever at her job. Once she'd even caught a former security guard committing a scam. He always came in very early, carrying a bag in which he kept his uniform. After changing into his uniform upstairs in the staff toilet, he'd put his civvy clothes into the bag and reverse the procedure every evening.

For a while, suits had been going missing from the menswear department. It was thought that men were going into the fitting room with perhaps three suits to try on and returning two, keeping the third on under their coat and leaving the store. Perhaps they knew how to remove the security tags. This had happened on several occasions. However, Miss Eden eventually discovered that the security guard was selling suits in a pub in Queen's Park, and so one day she searched his bag and found a suit, as well as his uniform. He had been getting out of the lift at the menswear department every morning and lifting a suit, before proceeding further up to the top floor.

After enjoying her lunch and a chat with Ian, Abi walked back along Glassford Street to Goodmans. She glanced further along across the road at the gay bar. She'd never actually seen anyone going in or out of there and she was curious. Did gay men look different, she wondered. Could you tell right away? She knew she was a bit innocent and naïve about some things.

And all right, she might be a wee bit eccentric sometimes. But that surely didn't make her stupid or mean she was losing her marbles.

Oh, Tom, she kept thinking.

The shop was busy as usual when she pushed open one of the glass doors and went in. There were metal gates in front of the glass doors that Mr McKay folded back on both sides like a concertina every morning. Every evening he clanged them shut and securely locked them. Mr McKay was standing talking to a customer at Books and Stationery, no doubt recommending one of the rows of novels on display. He had to spend a lot of time in his office every day, as she had to in her office, answering the phone and making phone calls, but he still tried to keep in touch with all the departments in person.

Today she couldn't be bothered tackling the stairs and instead caught the lift going up. She crushed in among a crowd of customers. The crush thinned out on each floor and only a couple of people were left to emerge on the third floor. She went up to the fourth floor. The lift door pinged and the soulless voice that always made her think of *Doctor Who*'s Cybermen announced, 'Fourth floor. Doors opening.'

She looked down the rather sombre corridor, doors breaking up the brown and cream wall at regular intervals. The parquet floor, dark brown with years of polish, clicked beneath her heels with metronome regularity as she headed towards the door at the end of the corridor. She cast a brief glance at the staff canteen on one side, as she passed the various offices, her tread slowing slightly as she neared Tom's office. The office was suspended in silence and Tom's empty chair reawakened the panic inside her that would never go away.

Every night she went home to his empty armchair beside the white marble fireplace, above which was the gilt-framed picture of Tom's father, the proud founder of Goodmans. The house, like the store, had belonged to Goodman Senior and she loved it as much as Tom did. The three padded armchairs and large sofa were all covered in pretty floral prints with a cushion on each chair and three on the settee, picking out one of the colours of the print material. At the moment, the cushions were in a warm rust colour. But there was also a set of pale green cushion covers in the linen cupboard. The ceiling was high, with ornate plasterwork in a pale cream like the curtains. The carpet was in a delicate shade of fawn, with a darker fawn fireside rug. It was a large room. So were the dining room and the kitchen and the five double bedrooms upstairs. The drawing room, however, was the most splendid-looking room, in true Victorian style. After a long tiring day at the store, she returned home and sank into her usual armchair beside the fire. The fire used to be alight and glowing with logs. Now there was an electric imitation coal thing in the fireplace. It looked completely out of place framed in such marble splendour, with the brass fender across the front and tall ornamental vases on the mantelpiece above.

Heaving herself up, she went through to the kitchen to make herself a cup of tea. She couldn't be bothered cooking anything and so she just absently crunched through a bowl of cereal. The evening stretched bleakly before her. She dreaded facing one of her *CSI: Miami* DVDs. She decided to go and visit the children. She felt a bit guilty at turning down the chance to be with them earlier. Douglas hadn't been pleased then. Maybe he'd be all right now.

It was a thought to trail away back into town. Even to travel there and back by taxi seemed daunting. Was she really getting old and tired? Sometimes she was tempted to sell the house in Huntershill and buy a flat in town. Near the store perhaps? That would save so much travelling to and fro. The house in Huntershill was so isolated, surrounded by trees and a wild garden of bushes and shrubs. Huntershill, of course, was famous because Thomas Muir had once lived in the area. He had been a reformer in the eighteenth century who had been transported to Australia, captured by pirates en route and ended up fighting in the French Revolution.

The sensible thing would be to sell up and buy a flat in the city. Moving house would be a terrible upheaval, though, and it would be such a wrench leaving this old house that had always meant home to the Goodmans.

She gave herself a mental shake, lifted the phone and dialled the taxi number. The roads were surprisingly quiet and she reached George Square more quickly than usual. It was with gathering unease that she stood with her ear close to the intercom, listening for Douglas or Minna's voice inviting her to come up to their flat. But it was the nanny's voice that crackled in her ear. The door opened and Abi went into the hall and took the lift up to the Benson's penthouse. She was relieved to find that Douglas and Minna had gone to a friend's house for dinner and the nanny was alone with the children.

'Just you leave them to me for a wee while,' Abi told the young woman. 'Go and watch the telly or something. Enjoy a rest.'

The nanny was only too happy to comply and wasted no time in disappearing away into her room.

The children were ready for bed but they danced around Abi in excitement.

'Sing us a song, Granny.'

'Tell us a story, Granny.'

'Give us a poem, Granny.'

After giving them a hug and a kiss, she settled herself in a chair and the children sat on the floor at her feet. She started off with one of their favourites.

Oh, it ain't gonna rain no more, no more,
It ain't gonna rain no more.

I'm on the bureau, the parish too,
And it ain't gonna rain no more.

After the children's giggles had subsided, she told them some stories of the mischief she had got up to when she was young, and how, at holiday time, she'd sailed 'doon the watter' with her mum and dad on a paddle steamer, and she sang, 'Sailing down the Clyde, sailing down the Clyde . . .'. She acted the paddles splashing round and had the youngsters copying her every move. After nearly an hour of talking and singing, she could see that they were ready to drop off to sleep, especially the twins. So she trooped them off to bed and tucked them in and kissed them goodnight. They were asleep before she reached the bedroom door on her way to tell the nanny she was returning home.

The worst of it was that, having had such a noisy, happy time with the children, the house at Huntershill seemed all the more silent and desolate. Not to worry, she told herself, in an effort to cheer herself up. It was off to *CSI: Miami* to meet her dear, kind Horatio again.

4

'For goodness' sake, Jimmy, not you again!' Miss Eden's voice strained with impatience. She had been ready to go home.

'Och, well,' the old man said, 'you know me, hen.'

'Yes, only too well. Give me back those jerseys and get away home.'

'Ah hinnae got a home, hen. That's why ah like tae get a decent bed in the polis office.' His lined face, ingrained with dirt, lit up with pleasant thoughts. 'The police gie me a great breakfast as well. They're no' bad lads.'

'Yes, but you are.' With a sigh, she used her mobile to call the police.

Mr McKay said irritably in passing, 'Don't let me see you in here again, you mucky old tramp. You're giving this place a bad name.'

Miss Eden noticed that Mr McKay had become unusually irritable recently. Indeed, he seemed very tense and anxious. She wondered what was wrong with him. She had a naturally curious, indeed suspicious, nature. It went with the job. Something was definitely wrong with Mr McKay. She had had enough to bother her today, however, without thinking about what was bothering Mr McKay. Earlier on, she'd seen a guy coming out of one of the fitting rooms with a shop suit on. She'd followed him downstairs and alerted the security guard.

By that time, the man had realised that they were on to him and at the door he suddenly dropped to the floor, gasping and groaning, his head flailing from side to side as he gripped his chest.

'Ah cannae feel ma left arm. God, ma chest. Ah cannae breathe for the pain.'

A crowd was quickly gathering as Miss Eden pushed her way to the front. She knew in her heart of hearts he was faking it but she needed to follow procedure, just in case.

She couldn't say, 'He's got a stolen suit on and he's just faking it', because in fact they couldn't be absolutely sure that he was faking it. The first-aider was called and she wasn't sure either. So the police and an ambulance were called and he was taken to the Royal Infirmary. She and the security guard and a policeman went with him in the ambulance and they all had to wait in a waiting area until the man was seen by a doctor. She explained to the nurse in attendance that he was wearing a stolen suit and, apart from anything else, they wanted it back. The nurse returned a couple of minutes later with the suit and said the doctor would be there as soon as possible to examine the patient.

They were standing in the long 'corporation green' corridor, discussing the shoplifter, nurses bustling to and fro into the various cubicles where a variety of patients waited, in various states of undress, for attention and medication.

Suddenly, the calm efficiency was destroyed as their charge burst out from behind the curtain, pushed the young policeman – from behind – headlong over a hospital gurney, and made a mad dash for freedom. He burst through the swing doors, his blue hospital gown billowing around him as he disappeared from view.

Miss Eden and the policeman dashed off in hot pursuit. They chased after him but lost him in the myriad of streets outside. Probably he was hiding in bushes somewhere. It was both exhausting and frustrating, and she felt glad when her duties for the day were finished and she was ready to leave. Until she'd seen old Jimmy snatch a pile of jumpers, of course. She waited until a policeman came and escorted a happy Jimmy away to his usual B. & B. at the police station. Then she left to walk up through George Square to Queen Street Station to catch a train to Springburn.

Within minutes, she was alighting at Springburn and crossing the road to her tenement flat. She had been born and brought up there and seen a lot of changes in the area – none of them good, in her opinion. Springburn used to have a heart, but since the motorway had cut through most of it, everything had changed. The atmosphere wasn't the same. It had none of the warmth and close community and neighbourliness that there had been in her parents' day and in the childhood that she remembered. To her at least, it had a strange, even a dangerous feel now. In the small covered shopping centre with its empty echoes, women had had their bags snatched by boys in hoodies. Or so she'd heard. Not that anything like that frightened her. She met with law-breakers of all kinds every day and was very confident and capable in dealing with them. Her black belt in karate helped, of course. She still attended a karate club every week.

Her flat had two bedrooms, a kitchen, a 'front room' as the sitting room had always been called, and a bathroom. Gone were the days when the lavatory was out on the landing and there was no hot water on tap. At least that had been a welcome change when the flats had been converted and modernised. The kitchen used to have a recessed or 'hole in the wall' bed. Now the bed was gone and in the recess was a round dining table and six chairs. Not that she entertained much. The table was rarely used for guests. It was bad policy to become friendly with the staff at work, and the neighbours were all out at their work during the day and she seldom even caught a glimpse of them. She supposed for most people, modern life meant a lonely life. One sign of this was the proliferation nowadays of dating agencies in newspapers and magazines and on television.

The karate club was her only social life, but it was a small club and as far as she knew, everyone was married. She'd had one or two couples from the club to dinner and had been invited back, but only a very few times. A single person always proved awkward at dinner parties or any other kind of social occasion. Sometimes she was tempted to try one of the dating agencies. Not that she was desperate for a man. She liked her job during the day. It was never dull and she enjoyed the weekly visit to the karate club and the television on other nights. It wasn't a bad life. She supposed, though, that it could be of extra interest to have a bit of companionship, especially as one got older. Someone to talk to about things. Her job, for instance, was so full of variety and interest, she often felt it would be nice to share her experiences with someone at the end of the day.

'You'll never guess what happened today,' she'd eagerly confide. And he would listen, fascinated. Then of course he'd tell her about his day. Yes, that would be enjoyable. Maybe she *would* try a dating agency. Of course, there could be dangers in that. It was the suspicious detective in her surfacing again. There had been cases of women being fooled by strangers they'd met through some of these dating agencies and ending up being robbed, raped or even murdered. She tried not to think in this suspicious way, but realised it was the penalty she had to pay for being such a good detective. She was very good at her job and she knew it, as well as everyone else.

This was the night for her karate club so, after having something to eat, she got ready, then made her way to the club. Once there, she bowed slightly from the waist as she entered the dojo. The sensei was already there, collecting fees. She hurried over and paid her mat fee, as the sensei called the class together.

The various grades shuffled together, organising in rows with senior grades to the right. The sensei called brusquely, 'Sei Sa', and the class kneeled in unison. The senior student then called out, ' Sensei nee rei', and as one, the class solemnly bowed heads to the floor in mutual respect. Then they sprang to their feet and immediately started into a vigorous warm-up.

She felt totally confident now. She felt she could tackle anything or anyone.

5

Sam Webster felt pleased and proud as he left the meeting. Mrs Goodman had praised him and his work, and rightly so. His toy department had become famous all over the country for its marvellously innovative toys. Mr McKay had echoed everything Mrs Goodman had said. His secret, of course, was the little old guy down in South Castle-on-Sea, who was a genius of an inventor. Sam had found him quite by accident when he had taken a wrong turning on his way to visit a toy wholesaler in South Castle. He found himself in a dead-end street and his attention was caught by a dingy shop front with a man working on a machine in the shadow beyond the grimy window. Sam decided it must be a workshop, not a retail business. On closer inspection, he felt intrigued by what the man was working on. It looked like some kind of robotic man. He'd felt excited as he watched and eventually he went inside. It turned out that the man made toys as a hobby. He just enjoyed inventing things and he didn't need to earn a living doing it. Long ago he had inherited money from his father. He wasn't interested in money. He was a real eccentric and Sam had blessed the day he'd found him. It had taken a bit of persuading and every ounce of charm he could muster to get the man to sign a contract to make toys for Goodmans.

'Think of all the pleasure you'll give to children' was one of his lines. 'Think how you'll stimulate children's curiosity and imagination' was another. 'You owe it to them,' he kept stressing.

So the inventor came up with each original model and then each model went into limited production. Another great thing about the deal was the fact that, because the inventor wasn't interested in money, costs could be kept to a minimum and profits were sky-high. No wonder Mrs Goodman et al. were so pleased with him.

A lot more than a good business deal resulted from the visit to South Castle-on-Sea. The B. & B. on the seafront that he'd booked into was owned by a very tasty lady, who had taken an immediate shine to him, and had invited him to share her bed, as well as providing an excellent breakfast. Of course, he supposed he wasn't a bad-looking guy. He was six foot four in height, with jet-black hair and dark eyes. His impressive appearance always helped in the business side of the job. It could also get him perks like Viv in the South Castle B. & B. He never went too far, of course. By that, he meant he was not like a sailor with a girl in every port. He succumbed to the occasional lady's advances, but only very occasionally. He loved his wife and was proud of his two daughters, who had recently started university. It could be lonely, however, being away from home so much, and he was often tempted.

Viv was a sexy lady devoid of any inhibitions. Sometimes he was almost shocked by her. At the same time he enjoyed himself. That situation was becoming a worry, though. He had never made a secret of being married, but now Viv was trying to persuade him to leave his wife and make South Castle his base. He reminded her that he'd been honest from the start and he'd made it clear that not only was he happily married, but he was employed by Goodmans of Glassford Street, an old-established Glasgow firm. At first, Viv said that they were only having a bit of fun. She was lonely, she said, and he was far from home and must be lonely too.

Now she had turned serious. Really serious. He tried to extricate himself from the situation but it only made things worse. Viv was a very determined woman. If she wanted something, she went after it, and there could be no doubt that she wanted him. He definitely could not go back to her B. & B. next time he visited South Castle. Yet it was necessary that he did visit South Castle on a regular basis to see his toy supplier. He began looking around the back streets for another place to stay. Somewhere he could hide away from Viv. It was annoying that he was forced to skulk around and it was difficult to be inconspicuous because he was six foot four. Difficult in any place, in any circumstances. He remembered a previous occasion when he had a lady on his arm and he spotted Miss Porter, a buyer in Ladies' Underwear, across the road. Fortunately she didn't see him. Very fortunately, because she knew his wife.

Eventually, he found a place and made a booking in advance for his next visit to South Castle. He usually texted Viv beforehand to tell her on what date and at what time he would be coming, but this time he certainly would not do that. He was especially attentive and loving to his wife, taking her a present from South Castle and telling her truthfully that he was very glad indeed to get back to Glasgow, and to her. She was so appreciative and so loving in return, it made him feel even more guilty. Moira was a good woman, and had always trusted him completely.

'Never again,' he vowed to himself. But of course, he'd promised himself that before. It was true what Viv said. There were times when he was lonely so far away from home or in some of the bleak and cheerless B. & B.s he'd stayed in. But it was his job and Goodmans was an excellent firm to work for. Mrs Goodman had also given Betty, his daughter who was a student at Glasgow University, a summer and weekend job in Books and Stationery. His other daughter, Alice, was at Edinburgh University and she worked in an Edinburgh supermarket in her spare time in order to make money for clothes and so on. Alice often said she wished she'd got a place at Glasgow University so that she too could have worked in Goodmans. Goodmans paid their staff exceptionally well.

He didn't know what would happen if Mrs Goodman retired, though. He supposed his job would be safe enough, but other staff members were worried about what would happen to them. Still, Mrs Goodman looked as if she had quite a few working years in her yet. She had a sense of humour, too.

'I'm having a senior moment,' she'd said to him recently. 'What the hell's your name again?'

'Webster, but no need to worry,' he'd assured her, 'I'm beginning to get these moments myself.'

Nobody could put anything past Mrs Goodman, though. She was nearly as good as Miss Eden at ferreting out anything wrong in any of the departments. If there was any neglect, laziness, inefficiency or dishonesty, she was on to it right away. (He suspected she wouldn't think much of adultery either.)

Not only were the wages excellent, but she was very good at giving time off if someone took ill or was pregnant. However, she was no soft mark and if she found out that someone was swinging the lead or cheating her in any way, she could immediately and ruthlessly sack them. But surely no matter what anyone found out about the odd flings he had while he was away from home, his job would be safe, because he had created such profits and such a good reputation for the toy department.

The big worry was that Moira would find out, or even Betty. While Betty worked in Books and Stationery, there was always the chance that if somebody – anybody – from

Goodmans found out what he got up to on his travels, it would reach Betty's ears. He would feel ashamed and embarrassed if that happened. And of course, even worse, Betty would be sure to tell her mother.

He must make certain that he was completely disentangled from Viv and he must never allow such a relationship to develop again. He had not, thank God, told Viv where he lived. Then he remembered that, of course, she knew he worked for Goodmans and Goodmans was situated in Glassford Street in Glasgow. Surely though, after he had turned her down and then not contacted her again, she would realise that the affair was definitely over. And she would never be so foolish as to contact him at work. He did receive a great deal of mail but it was all on business matters, and usually opened first by his assistant in Toys. He kept assuring himself that Viv would not be so foolish as to write to him. What would be the point? He'd told her it was over and no way, and for no reason, would he ever leave his wife.

Yet still his anxiety grew.

6

Jenny managed to raise her hand as he bent over her. She touched his receding hair.

'You're going grey, Norman. That's with all the worry you've had with me. I'm so sorry, dear.'

'Don't be daft.' He tried to laugh. 'What does it matter what colour my hair is? All I care about is you.' He kissed her gently on the brow. 'I want you to get better. That's the important thing.'

She sighed. 'We both know that's not possible, dear. You know and I know what the doctor said.'

Oh, he knew what the doctor said, all right. He had sent her home from the hospital to die in her own bed.

'I'm sorry, Mr McKay,' he'd said, 'there's really nothing more we can do for your wife. She has only another few months, perhaps only a few weeks.'

He'd made enquiries at the clinic at the other end of the town, however, and been told what this new drug could do. What miracles it could perform. Or at least he thought of it as a miracle, if they could save Jenny or even just prolong her life and make it pain-free. Despite the painkillers she was taking at the moment, she was still suffering.

He gathered her in his arms and rocked her gently, close to his chest, praying that he could hold back his tears, because it upset Jenny so much when she saw him weeping. Later, he wept silently in the bathroom, his chest heaving, his eyes screwed shut. For years they had been so happy together. She was his first and only love. Every evening she used to drive to Goodmans to pick him up, then drive him home. Except once a week (sometimes twice), when they would go to a restaurant for dinner, and he would have a couple of glasses of wine. He would have done without the wine because she couldn't drink and drive. However, she always insisted that he needed the wine to help him relax after a busy day in Goodmans.

If they went straight home, she'd make him sit down and enjoy a glass of wine while she attended to the evening meal. Afterwards they would both relax before the fire and he'd tell her all about his day at Goodmans. They often had a good laugh together but still he couldn't help asking, 'Are you sure I'm not boring you with all my talk about what happens at Goodmans?'

'Of course not,' she'd assure him. 'I enjoy hearing all your stories. I really do.'

She would tell him about her day as well. Then they would watch the news on television and *Coronation Street* (Jenny's favourite), and perhaps *The Bill*. Or *Rebus*. They both liked *Rebus* and had read most of Ian Rankin's books. Later they'd enjoy a hot milky drink and a biscuit before snuggling up together in bed. Nearly every night they made love.

Since Jenny had taken ill, of course, she had not been well enough for any love-making. He only ever held her in his arms and whispered over and over again how much he had always loved her and always would.

He couldn't bear the thought of not being able to give her the chance of being saved by the new drug. He *had* to get her to that clinic. He *had* to get the money from somewhere. No use trying the bank. He already had an enormous loan. They wouldn't give him one penny more. He knew that because he'd tried.

Now, when he made several journeys every evening to the bank with the takings from Goodmans, he had begun to think about how that money could work the miracle for Jenny. He had never, never in his whole life before, had one dishonest thought. Over the years, he had worked his way up in Goodmans and prided himself that he had always been a good, hard worker, conscientious and honest. Mrs Goodman appreciated his conscientiousness and his honesty. He could not betray her trust and let her down.

And yet . . . and yet . . . Every night he was tormented by having to handle all that money. If he did defraud the firm, how could he manage it? There was not only Mrs Goodman's sharp attention to every aspect of the business. There was Miss Eden. Nothing dishonest ever escaped her eagle eye. It had to be done in a way that meant he would not be caught or even suspected. He had not only to get Jenny cured at the clinic, he had always to be there for her, and she, of all people, must never find out what he had done. She would feel she was to blame and it would distress her so much. The thing was, though, he couldn't think how he could steal the money. The more he thought about Jenny, the more desperate he became, the more feverishly he tried to think of a way, a safe way, to commit the crime. It was driving him mad. He couldn't sleep at night now for trying to figure out how he could not only get the money, but also get away with it.

He struggled to calm down, or at least to look calm and normal, every day at work. Already he thought Miss Eden was giving him the occasional suspicious glance. And even Mrs Goodman's sharp eyes were piercing through his façade of normality. Or was it just his guilty conscience making him imagine that people suspected he was up to something? He struggled to control nervous habits he had recently acquired,

7

Abi gazed at the outward façade of the Scottish Parliament. John had told her that Enric Miralles, the architect, had studied in Glasgow and Edinburgh and was influenced by Charles Rennie Macintosh. She thought Charles Rennie Macintosh was a genius and some of his buildings were masterpieces. The Glasgow School of Art, for instance. But this? She shook her head. She couldn't see Charles Rennie Macintosh in this. This was a complex of buildings with what looked like bamboo rods all over the walls outside. John said it was oak latticing. John loved everything about the Parliament.

Inside there was, in her opinion, a rather confusing and unwelcoming feeling, which wasn't helped, of course, by the security. She had to empty some things into a tray. Then her handbag went through and then she walked through another part. It had once pinged several times until she'd had to be frisked. She had forgotten that she had her door key clipped on to the waistband of her skirt. It was all very embarrassing and humiliating. Further in, she was under the vaults. Historically, the vault was to hold up your tower, but also so that invaders couldn't burn your house out by setting a fire on the ground floor. Under her feet was Kemnay granite from north-east Scotland and Caithness slab from the far north-east of the

Scottish mainland. But what a mix-up it all was inside and out. Everything was over the top. But John said it was meant to be the reverse of the Modernist doctrine of 'less is more' to 'more is different'.

She looked around for John's secretary but couldn't see her. Of course, she was a bit early. She was already carrying a bag of cakes from a bakery on the Royal Mile. Nevertheless, she decided to visit the Parliament shop while she was waiting for John's secretary, and make some more purchases. She couldn't remember the secretary's name. But she'd recognise her when she saw her, she hoped. The shop sold bottles of special wine and delicious fudge and chocolates and other sweets. The children would enjoy them. It would be an excuse for her to visit them. Not that she needed an excuse. She'd taken the day off work to come and have lunch with John, and then listen to him for a while in the debating chamber, before returning home in the afternoon. Douglas Benson was delighted that she'd taken the day off and he would certainly have no complaints about her visiting the children.

After filling another carrier bag with shopping, she returned to wander around the main hall area and the lobby, tossing critical glances up at the upturned boat shapes and shoals of fish and leaf forms. All extremely over the top, in her opinion.

Still no sign of the secretary. She began to wonder a little fearfully if indeed she had forgotten what the woman looked like and she was already there among the crowd of people milling around. Then she caught sight of John's tall, slim figure. She had to smile to herself. Not that long ago, before he had entered Parliament, he went about in jeans and baggy pullovers and his hair was long and untidy. Now he wore a smart suit, shirt and tie. His hair was cut short-back-and-sides but he still had a bush of curls on top.

She waved to him and he came striding over to give her a welcoming hug. He had always been a demonstrative, affectionate boy.

'Where's your secretary, son?' Abi asked. 'Did I miss her?'

'No, she hasn't come in today. I don't know what's wrong. She hasn't phoned in to say. It's not like her. I phoned her place just now and got no reply. But of course she's often away doing research or other odd jobs for me. Anyway, how are you, Mum? You're looking very smart. Quite glamorous, in fact. Here, give me your shopping bags. We can put them up in my office before we go for lunch.'

She didn't even like his office. It was long and narrow and didn't look at all comfortable or adequate. But John loved working here, anywhere and everywhere in the Parliament, in fact. He assured her that everybody did.

In the office, he dumped her message bags on the secretary's desk, repeating in puzzlement, 'It's not like her not to phone.'

'Oh, I bet she'll phone later. It's early yet.'

He didn't look convinced. 'Anyway, come on. You must be hungry.'

'Yes, I'll enjoy a bit of lunch. But the best thing about today, son, is seeing you and I'm looking forward to a wee while in the debating chamber. I hope you get a chance to speak.'

'Don't worry. I'll have something to say, all right.'

They made their way to the restaurant and settled down at one of the tables. While supping enthusiastically at his carrot and coriander soup, John said, 'It makes me mad when I think of all that's going on just now. What a bloody mess – and I mean literally – there is in Iraq just now. Saddam has no weapons of mass destruction, so that was Tony Blair lying for a start. We didn't go in to defend ourselves. Or the Iraqis for that matter. Nowadays the ordinary Iraqis can't even go out to a market for food and other essentials without risking death. I was speaking to a woman the other day. Her cousin had to go out and try to buy some petrol and was killed. He leaves a family of young children now with no food or heating at home.'

'Poor things.' Abi's face creased up with sympathy. 'Life's so short at the best of times, but now there's so much killing and cruelty everywhere.'

'The laugh is,' John said, with bitter seriousness, 'the ones that *do* have the weapons are Britain and America. America has even used them. Not once, but twice.'

Abi shuddered, remembering the photographs she'd seen of children with the patterns of their clothing burned into their skin. Huge, flattened, desolate areas that had once been cities full of people going about their business in shops and offices and at home, looking after their families, had been destroyed in seconds.

'Is that all right, Mum?'

Abi felt confused for a few moments until she realised John was meaning the steak pie and chips she was eating.

'Yes, delicious thanks, son.'

'How's Benson behaving himself?'

'Oh, the usual. He's trying to keep me out of the shop as much as possible. His latest ploy is to try and get me to babysit the children during the day. I'm always tempted by that. But I try to resist and only go in the evenings to see the children.'

'He'll love you coming through to Edinburgh, then.'

'Oh yes. He always says, "Why don't you stay with John for a few days?"'

'You know you're always welcome at my flat, Mum. The spare bedroom is yours any time you want it.'

'I know, dear, but I need to keep an eye on what he's doing in the store.'

'Could you go a pudding, Mum? They've got chocolate sponge.'

'No thanks. That pie filled me up. Just a cup of tea will do me fine. Anyway, dear, is it not time you were taking your seat in the chamber?'

'I've still time for a quick coffee.'

Over coffee, he again brought up the question of Julie, his secretary, saying, 'Still no word from her and she's got my mobile number as well. I don't understand it. She's normally so conscientious.'

'There'll be some perfectly good explanation. Try not to worry, John.'

He nodded, and eventually pushed back his chair and rose.

'I'd better go. You stay and finish your tea.'

He bent down and kissed her.

'Thanks for coming, Mum. It's great to see you.'

She made her way up to the debating chamber, where several people – including what looked like a party of schoolchildren – were already seated. Meetings of Parliament took place every Wednesday afternoon and all day on Thursdays. People came on non-business days as well, just to have a look around.

At least she liked all the console desks like little pulpits carved in sycamore and oak in the chamber. John said the chamber was less confrontational than Westminster, where the two sides were two sword-lengths apart. Now a Labour man was arguing about how Scotland could never be financially independent. It would always have a deficit in its budget.

John reminded the man that secret papers from the 1970s that had been deliberately withheld from the Nationalists had now been released to the public and clearly stated that in the seventies, the government at the time knew that – as the Nationalists had always claimed and still claimed – Scotland would be heavily in surplus. Scotland would be able to keep all its wealth, including North Sea oil revenues, if the country was not a region, but an independent country.

'The argument for wealth in a small country,' John said, 'is not something we're hypothesising. You can see it in Norway, in Finland, in Sweden, in Luxembourg, which is a fifth of the size of Scotland. These countries are among the richest in Europe.'

Abi was definitely going to vote Scottish Nationalist at the next election. John had inspired and persuaded her. She wouldn't mention this to Douglas Benson, of course. He would really believe she'd gone out of her mind if he found that out. Anyway, it was none of his or anyone's business whom she voted for. She thoroughly enjoyed her visit to Edinburgh. Glasgow was her first love, but it was a pleasure to walk up the Royal Mile, as long as she ignored the outside of the Scottish Parliament.

The Royal Mile was full of interest. For instance, across the road was White Horse Close and the White Horse Inn. The Close was the original stables at Holyrood House and the Close was named after the white palfrey belonging to Mary, Queen of Scots. After that, it was the Jacobite headquarters during the '45 rebellion, and then an inn and terminus of stagecoaches to London. It was amazing to think that the journey took eight days in 1745.

The Royal Mile stretched right up to the Castle, passing two of the oldest houses in Edinburgh – one where the writer Daniel Defoe once lived and another that had been John Knox's house. Abi didn't go right up to the Castle, but turned off to make her way to Waverley Station, where she caught a train back to Glasgow.

Although she liked Edinburgh and was fascinated by its history, her heart belonged to her native city. As soon as the train pulled in at Queen Street Station, she felt at home. She was looking forward to being with the children. It wasn't yet closing time for the store and so Douglas and Minna would still be at work.

George Square was busy. Some people were sitting on the seats; others, obviously tourists, were taking pictures of the imposing City Chambers, or the Cenotaph, or the statues. Abi crossed over to the building in which the Benson penthouse was situated high above the Square.

The nanny welcomed her in and gratefully disappeared into the nether regions and left her on her own with the children. After hugs and kisses, Abi was touched by the wide-eyed expectant expressions on their little faces. She knew, and they knew, that nowhere else and from nobody else did they hear such stories and songs. Once she got them settled around her and they were happily sucking the sweets that she'd brought, she began to sing:

My wee lad's a sodger,
He lived in Maryhill.
He gets his pay on a Saturday night,
And he buys a half a gill.
He goes to the church on Sunday,
A half an hour late,
Pulls the buttons off his shirt,
And puts them in the plate.

Then, to the clapping of hands and with the children doing their best to join in:

There's a big ship sailing down the ali, ali, o,
The ali, ali, o, the ali, ali, o.
There's a big ship sailing down the ali, ali, o,
On the nineteenth of September.

After that, there was much giggling as Abi sang in broad Scots:

43

Twelve an' a tanner a bottle,
That's what it's costin' today.
Twelve an' a tanner a bottle,
Takes aw the pleasures away.
For if you want a wee drappie,
You've got to spend aw you've got.
How can a fella be happy,
When happiness costs such a lot?

Then the enthusiastic clapping started again, and the children joined in with:

There were rats, rats, with bowler hats and spats,
In the store, in the store.
There were rats, rats, with bowler hat and spats,
In the Co-operative store.
My eyes are dim, I cannot see,
I have not got my specs with me.
I have not got my specs with me.

By this time, the children were falling about in hilarity, and so she thought she'd better tell them a quiet, more sensible (and the nanny would say more suitable) story. But the children wanted to hear 'silly songs' as they called them. They didn't know what the words meant half the time. She thought it was the unusualness and, she suspected, the naughtiness of the songs that fascinated the children and excited their laughter.

The nanny must have quite a problem trying to keep their attention on Timothy Tiptoes or Brer Rabbit. If the nanny tried to tell them stories at all. Douglas and Minna certainly never bothered. Minna might have paid more attention to the children but Douglas dragged her out socialising so much. No wonder he wanted to take over Goodmans. He spent money as if he'd invented it. The city's most expensive restaurants knew him as a regular customer, as did the nightclubs and bars. He and Minna were not trendy youngsters and so at least they avoided the many places where young people went. She'd seen the crowds of youngsters arriving in town to mill around the city streets at ten o'clock in the evening, just ready at that (to her) late hour to start their noisy rounds of nightclubs and discos.

No, Douglas and Minna had their own clubs and hotels that catered for the more mature, upmarket clientele. Expensive places. Though Douglas kept telling her that what he planned, or would like to happen, at the store was all for the good, cutting expenses, expanding, and so on. It was all for the good of the store, he said. That's all he cared about, he kept telling her. She didn't believe a word of it. The first thing he'd do, she was sure, was buy a big house with lots of land and live like a lord. He'd soon fritter away any profits he would manage to make in Goodman's. He didn't care about the place, only himself.

What a worry it all was for her. If only John would take over, but John was just not a businessman. Never had been. Politics was his thing. He had been clever at school, and then at university, and always, from the very start, he'd dreamed about getting into politics. He'd told her it was one of the happiest days of his life, if not *the* happiest, when he was elected as an MSP.

She would never, could never, spoil John's happiness. She would just have to hang on in there as long as she could. And try to find another solution.

8

Miss Eden was never at ease in the Sheriff Court. She spent a lot of time there, if whoever she'd caught pled not guilty. It always made her feel a bit afraid, because whoever was in the dock was seeing her giving her evidence as she was, without any disguises. They didn't know where she lived but they knew where she worked. The funny thing was, though, she often became the best bosom buddy of the people she'd stopped, and they treated her with respect. The men at least, seldom the women. Women could be nasty, especially the young ones. She'd often caught them with a weapon of some sort ready to use on her. One woman had tried to stab her with a pair of scissors. She'd just stopped another in time, as she was trying to throw pepper in her face.

She'd been in court most of the day and still had to return to Goodmans for another hour or two. She had barely changed into an old coat and headscarf and made her way down to the first floor, when she saw a woman slipping a jumper into a Goodmans bag, which obviously held some other purchases she'd paid for earlier. She signalled to the security guard and they waited until the woman left the shop. Outside in the street, she stopped the woman, told her she had reason to believe she had stolen goods in her possession, and led her back inside and upstairs to the manager's office. Never before had she seen such an extreme reaction. The woman was absolutely distraught, shaking violently with fear as she pleaded – at one point actually down on her knees – for them not to tell her husband.

Eventually, after she had returned the stolen jumper, Mr McKay let her go. This was unheard of and Miss Eden was not only taken back, but annoyed. What was the use of her working hard and keeping so eagle-eyed every minute of the day, and being so conscientious in every way at her job, if thieves could just walk away like that? If Mrs Goodman had been there, it would have been a different story. Mrs Goodman was a stickler for the rules. Normally, so was Mr McKay. She didn't know what had come over him recently. He was like a different man. She was beginning to distrust him. Something she had not imagined she could ever feel. Not for Mr McKay. But to let somebody walk free like that! It was encouraging crime. If word got around there would be thieves flocking to Goodmans from all over the place. She felt aggrieved. Her work was difficult enough as it was, without the manager making it worse.

She had barely returned downstairs again, when she saw a woman acting suspiciously. Just my luck, she thought. Another woman, of course. Men would say when they were caught, 'Fair cop.' Women tried to run or fight back. However, the woman saw her and recognised her and decided not to try anything. She left the store empty-handed.

No sooner had that happened than she spied a man putting on a camel coat in the menswear department and calmly leaving the department still wearing the coat. She followed him, stopped him outside and escorted him back inside the store. There he said he needed the bathroom. He was desperate, he said.

'OK, the security guard will take you upstairs to the toilet.'

Then to the security guard, 'Take him up to the toilet and stay with him.'

But the security guard stood outside the door. As soon as she saw him standing there, she called out, 'I told you to stay with him!'

'He can't get out unless he passes me. We're three flights up.'

Nevertheless, she pushed her way past the guard and into the toilet. The toilet window was open and the man had gone. She looked out the window to the lane below, and saw him writhing in agony on the ground. There were drainpipes all around the building and grease was always put on the pipes to prevent people getting up them at night. Obviously, when the man had got on to the pipe to climb down, he slid down unexpectedly, and rapidly.

'By the looks of him,' she told the security guard, 'he's got a broken leg. Phone for an ambulance, as well as the police.'

She waited with the man, trying to make him as comfortable as possible until the ambulance came. Then she followed the usual procedure and went with him to the hospital. She was never nasty, never used unnecessary violence. She always treated the thieves as human beings. She supposed that was why most of them respected her and even became quite friendly. If they saw her in the street, they'd call out, 'Hello there, hen.'

After returning to her office and filling in the necessary reports, she told Mr McKay that she was going off duty. Then she thankfully went for the train. It was good to get home and put her feet up and have a cup of tea and a read of the evening newspaper. She never ate much at night. She enjoyed a good meal at the staff canteen at lunchtime. It was store policy that she didn't sit with any of the staff or become too familiar with them. This was a bit difficult at times, but it was a rule that had to be adhered to. Sometimes she had to deal with staff dishonesty. Spot checks on staff handbags had to be made. Sometimes she had to depend on information from staff, but even that had to be on a businesslike level.

It meant, of course, that she often felt a bit isolated and lonely, especially when she had to sit alone at home as well. Thoughts of a dating agency came into her mind again. In the paper tonight there was a page with a list of people seeking friends or partners. This wasn't an agency, just people like herself needing a bit of company, she supposed. Some of the adverts were from men wanting to meet men. One she noticed said, 'Gentleman aged sixty. Loyal, sincere. Hobbies – walking, swimming. Would like to meet similar gentleman for friendship, holiday. Can travel.' And a box number was given.

One from a woman said, 'Woman graduate seeks gentleman to share interests. Classical music, ballet, theatre.'

What could she say if she put in an advert? She didn't think it would be a good idea to say that she was a detective. That would put a lot of men off. Unless the man was a policeman, of course. But did she want to go out with a policeman? She didn't think so. Their jobs would be too similar. It might work, but at the moment at least, she felt she'd had enough to do with crime and criminals. Something or somebody different to take her mind off the job might be a better idea and more successful.

Another problem could be her lack of a degree. She had done well at school and had passed all her Higher exams. Then she'd gone to a special college in England where she'd trained as a detective. Common sense was important, but how to stop thieves, how to do statements, go to court, and so on – you had to learn all that. And you must know the law. She'd started in another, bigger store at first, assisting the detective there. Eventually she'd got a better job and a bigger salary at Goodmans.

None of that would be of much use, she felt, in attracting a man. Maybe not being a graduate wouldn't matter so much. It was the detective business. Perhaps she could just say she worked in a department store and it would be taken for granted she was a sales assistant. Or, at the advert stage at least, she needn't mention anything about a job. So what could she say? How could she describe herself?

She wasn't a woman who liked to boast. She didn't believe she was anything special – unless at her job. She *was* special at that. Otherwise she was pretty ordinary. Hobbies? Karate was the only one. That might not make her sound very appealing to a man either. So what on earth could she say? 'Very ordinary woman seeks nice, respectable man for company.' Oh dear.

Unless she made something up. She couldn't do that either. She was, and always had been, an absolutely honest person. That was essential for her work. Everything always came back to her work. Always her work. It was as if there was nothing else in her life – nothing else to her – but her job.

That was what depressed her. She liked her work and wouldn't want to change it for any other. Nevertheless, there surely had to be another side to her life. All work and no play . . ., as the saying went.

Eventually she wrote, 'Hard-working but lonely lady in her mid forties seeks respectable gentleman in his fifties or sixties for companionship.' Or should she put friendship? Could companionship be misunderstood? Before she got so fed up and abandoned the whole idea, she lifted the phone, dialled the newspaper's number and gave them the advert.

Then she had to go and search out the tranquillisers her late mother used to take. There were some left in the sideboard drawer. After her mother died, she had meant to throw out all the medication that was left but had forgotten. Now she needed one of those tranquillisers. Otherwise she'd never settle, even to watch her favourite TV programme, far less calm herself to sleep at bedtime. It was so unlike her to get so uptight and anxious about anything.

Of course, there might be no replies to the advert. Most men, she imagined, would be looking for a much younger woman. Somebody young and vivacious and glamorous. She was none of those things. Still, she tried to tell herself, there might be a few lonely mature men who would prefer an older, more sensible woman.

She could hardly wait next day to buy an evening paper. And there it was, her advert. Thank God it was just under a box number and she could not be identified. Then another thought struck her. What if she got a reply and it was from an elderly employee at Goodmans? How embarrassing that would be! Of course, she would remain anonymous because she wouldn't – couldn't – reply to him. She found herself looking at all the older men in the shop. There were a few who looked ready for retirement – two in the menswear department and one in Soft Furnishings and another in Electrical. But they were probably happily married. They all looked happy enough.

She struggled to put the whole thing out of her mind and concentrate on the job. Then she spied a good-looking, well-dressed man walk in and, in a confident, businesslike way, collect a pile of suits from one of the racks. None of the assistants questioned him, thinking he was a buyer.

She had to really spring through the department to get near to him and see what was going to happen next. She hardly had time to call to the security guard to follow her, before the man reached the door and was outside.

'Excuse me,' she called to him as soon as she reached him. 'You are—'

He began to run then and she and the security guard belted after him. But the security guard was too overweight for running and it was she who caught up with him. It was most unusual for a man to fight her but he did. Big mistake. He

51

swung round towards her, grabbing her jacket roughly as he tried to shove her back. She whipped her right hand across, grabbed his hand at the wrist with a soft twist, while pushing his elbow with her left, and spun him round into a wrist lock. She stabbed the edge of her foot onto the back of his knee joint to bring him to his knees in front of her. Grabbing his hair, she bent him back like a strongbow.

'Enough,' she said quietly into his ear. 'Let's just go quietly upstairs before this becomes really painful.'

By this time the security guard had reached them and they were able to continue with the usual routine. The man accompanied her back to the store and up to the manager's office like a lamb.

A lot of time was always taken up waiting for the police and also writing up reports, and she had just got back to the ground floor when she noticed a part-time member of staff going into the fitting room with a pile of underwear. She was a nice wee girl who was studying at Jordanhill College, and of course there were times when staff could make purchases. All the same, there was not another member of staff on duty at the fitting room, and she felt a bit annoyed. She'd so often told the managers of every department always to have someone in attendance at the fitting rooms. Eventually she saw the girl come out and replace a pile of underwear on the counter. On this occasion, she didn't like to – indeed felt guilty about doing it, but rules were rules.

'Just a minute, dear,' she said to the girl. 'Could you come back into the fitting room with me for a minute?'

At the same time, she signalled for an assistant to come too. There she asked the girl to take off her top and skirt. The girl immediately burst into tears and before the top and skirt came off, it was obvious that she would be seen to be wearing several sets of Goodmans underwear.

She was immediately dismissed, and next day the girl's

mother was on the phone demanding to know why her daughter had been sacked. But it was decided that it was up to the girl to explain to her mother.

Then one of the customers complained to the manager that an assistant in the shoe department was smelling of drink. A check was made and some of the other staff agreed. 'Yes, she's always reeking of alcohol.'

The problem was to catch her drinking on the premises or bringing drink into the shop. This was proving very difficult. The assistant denied everything, of course. She was watched and searched several times. Her bag was checked. Nothing. She never even went out at lunchtime but always ate in the staff canteen. She did, however, go to the toilet. This was perfectly natural, but her detective's instinct told Miss Eden to go to the toilet after the assistant, stand up on the seat and search in the high, old-fashioned cistern. Sure enough, a carefully wrapped bottle of whisky was discovered – which meant another sacking.

Big problems – and trouble – were to come as a result of that sacking, though.

9

Tucking her hair behind her ears, Abi peered down at the *TV Times* on her lap. Nothing much on tonight. She got up to gaze out of the window. The light from the standard lamp in the room barely touched the darkness, the ghostly swaying shapes of the trees and high bushes. The sight increased her depression to the point of fear. Maybe she shouldn't keep the curtains open like this. Then she felt ashamed. She had never been a coward. She sat down again.

There was a programme on politics but she had no interest in politics except for anything John had to say or do. Indeed, she was completely disillusioned with the whole bunch of politicians. Except for John, of course. John was one hundred per cent honest and sincere. So much so that she had decided to vote Scottish Nationalist next time. A sudden loud creaking noise made her jump. But it was only the trees straining in the wind. There was quite a storm brewing. Better to shut the curtains to keep out the cold, and to muffle the sound of the windows rattling. At one time, they'd had a lovely big log fire in the sitting room. Now it was this artificial coal thing that looked so out of place in the beautiful big marble fireplace. It had just two electric bars and was not nearly enough to heat such a high-ceilinged room. It was at times like this that she wished she lived in a little flat somewhere in the centre of the city. Yet what a wrench it would be to leave the house she'd shared for so many years with Tom. It would feel as if she was deserting him for ever. Losing every last trace of him. Here, she could still imagine him relaxing on the big easy chair opposite her, his long legs stretched out. Sometimes, while they were chatting, he'd lean forward and toss a log on to the fire.

Thank God she could keep busy all day at the store. She couldn't stand being alone like this. Depression kept creeping up on her. Sometimes, of course, she kept too busy at the store and exhausted herself.

One of the women buyers had noticed and said, 'Forgive me for saying this, Mrs Goodman, but you look as if you're overdoing things. You haven't even taken any holidays this year.'

But what was the use of going away somewhere, anywhere, on her own? And it was into winter now. It would be even worse in some seaside town at this time of year on her own. She certainly didn't feel inclined to travel abroad any more.

Thinking of the buyer and then seaside towns made Mr Webster come into her mind. He travelled all over the place, including seaside towns. One in particular was South Castle-on-Sea, where he had some old man invent the marvellous toys that were in such demand in the toy department. An idea was beginning to occur to her. She had long been curious about the inventor. It would be perfectly reasonable and understandable if she wanted to meet him. And what better way than to go with Mr Webster to South Castle? That way she could have company and be well looked after. Mr Webster was an excellent driver and a nice friendly man. He often spoke proudly about his daughters. Then there would be all the benefits of the sea air. Mr Webster would know all the best places to have coffee and meals on the journey down, as well as the best place to stay in South Castle. Abi had never learned to drive and couldn't be bothered nowadays with trains and buses. She was beginning to feel her age, although there was no way she would ever admit it to anyone.

The more she thought about the journey in Mr Webster's comfortable car and the bracing air of South Castle, the more cheered she began to feel. She would speak to him tomorrow. He couldn't refuse to take her. She was his boss, after all.

As it turned out, she couldn't speak to him the next day because he was up north visiting a wholesaler there. But he was due back in a couple of days and so she would speak to him then.

'When are you off to South Castle-on-Sea again, Mr Webster?' she asked him on his return.

'In a couple of weeks.'

Good, she thought, that would give her something to look forward to.

'I've decided to come with you on this occasion, Mr Webster. I'd like to meet your wonderful inventor.'

He looked not just surprised, but shocked.

'Are you sure?' he managed eventually.

'Why shouldn't I?'

He smiled and looked more like his normal self again.

'You are always so busy here. I'm truly amazed that you can spare the time, Mrs Goodman.'

'Oh, don't worry. I know how to delegate. And the change will do me good. Not that there's anything wrong with me,' she hastened to add. 'But variety is the spice of life, they say, and a visit to South Castle-on-Sea will add a bit of variety to my working day.'

'We can't get back on the same day, you understand. I've business to do with . . .'

'Of course! Stay as long as you have to. The store won't suddenly collapse if I'm not here for a few days.'

'Right.' He smiled again. 'I'll make the necessary arrangements.'

She had been talking to him in the toy department. Now she returned to her office with a spring in her step. John kept telling her she ought to get out and about more, and as usual, he was right. She phoned him. Not to tell him about her proposed visit to South Castle-on-Sea, but just to say she was coming to Edinburgh for one of her visits to have lunch with him and enjoy her usual short spell in the gallery of the debating chamber. She looked forward to surprising him and she hoped he would be pleased with her news.

One thing was for sure, Douglas Benson would be delighted to get rid of her when she went off to South Castle-on-Sea. He would encourage her to stay as long as she liked. Not because, like John, he wanted the visit to do her good. Only because he'd have free run of the store while she was away.

She went over that evening to announce her news. Every time she passed through George Square, whether in a taxi or on foot, she could not help admiring the City Chambers building. It had taken seven years to build and craftsmen from places as far away as France and Italy had helped to build it. She had often been inside the building too, sometimes at events to which she had been invited. At other times she had taken a guided tour or just gone in and looked around by herself. By now, she knew most of the guides and other staff. She never failed to feel a sense of awe at the imposing and beautiful marble staircase and the wonderful Venetian mosaic that the roof was composed of. It had a million and a half different pieces of mosaic, half-inch cubes, each of which had been inserted by hand. However, most of the interior decoration was carried out by Glasgow men employed by Glasgow firms.

In the summer in her lunch hour, she often sat on one of the benches in George Square admiring the flowerbeds or the statues. It always annoyed her, though, that the statue of Sir

Walter Scott was so much bigger, higher and more imposing than that of Robert Burns. (It was the same in Edinburgh.) She'd read somewhere that there wouldn't have been a statue of the poet at all if it had not been for the citizens of Glasgow, who managed to raise the money for it themselves.

The Benson penthouse looked down on the Square. Sometimes when musical or other events were held there, it was fascinating to watch everything going on from such a good vantage point.

Douglas and Minna had friends in for dinner, and when she arrived, give them their due, both Minna and Douglas invited her to join the company for a meal. She refused, however.

'Thank you, but I have eaten. I'll just go to the nursery and spend some time with the children. I'll see you both at the store tomorrow.'

As usual, the children were delighted to see her and the usual cry went up, 'Tell us a story, Grandma. Sing us a song.'

John said she should write a book with all the songs and poems and her made-up stories in it.

'If you don't, they'll probably all die out,' he told her. 'It's only the likes of you that keep them going. And your stories are really good, Mum. They deserve to be published.'

She had laughed at him. All her songs and poems were silly and daft things that very few people nowadays would even understand. And half the stories she made up were equally daft. Perhaps a few elderly Glasgow people, especially people who had lived through the war, would recognise some of the silly songs. But that was all.

She remembered all the ones her mother used to sing to her.

Whenever there's an air raid on
You can hear me cry,
An aeroplane, an aeroplane, away up a kye,

58

So don't run helter skelter,
And don't run after me,
You'll no' get in my shelter,
For it's far too wee.

The children always enjoyed another one, particularly.

Wee chukie birdie,
To lo lo,
Laid an egg on the window sole,
The window sole began to crack,
And wee chukie birdie roared and grat.

After telling them a story about a clever fairy, she noticed them getting so sleepy that they could hardly keep their eyes open, and so she ended by singing softly:

Show me the way to go home,
I'm tired and I want to go to bed.
I had a little drink about an hour ago,
And it's gone right to my head.
No matter where I roam,
Over land or sea or foam,
You can always hear me singing this song,
Show me the way to go home.

A book indeed! She smiled to herself as she slipped away from the house. John had such faith in her. For a start, a lot of people nowadays would think her songs and stories were unsuitable for children. Well, they had never done her generation any harm. Children were too coddled nowadays. They weren't even supposed to compete with each other in school sports in case those who lost would suffer trauma or something or other. What nonsense! Life was competitive.

How did the powers that be think they were preparing children to face life? She pitied teachers because they were not even allowed to raise their voices to children now. One of the customers she'd spoken to the other day in Hosiery was a teacher and had told her that when she tried to correct a youngster in her class, he refused to be told anything and said cheekily to her, 'I know my rights!' Another, who had been caught stealing, sneered, 'You can't do anything. I'm under age.'

In her day, if you were cheeky to the teachers (and who would dare?), you got the belt. And if you told your mother that you'd got belted, your mother would say, 'You must have done something to deserve it.'

And she would box your ears for good measure. It had never done her any harm. And you learned everything by rote. The arithmetic tables, especially. As a result, she'd never forgotten them. That kind of learning was not fashionable now – not PC, to use the in-phrase. As a result, she'd read that many students were leaving school unable even to spell or understand the most basic maths. Fancy!

Well, one thing was certain – university or not, they wouldn't get a job at Goodmans of Glassford Street. Not while she had anything to do with it. As for cheek or any lack of politeness, any bad manners – especially to customers, God forbid – it would be an immediate sacking.

She got a taxi home and, as she went into the dark and empty Victorian house, it was like stepping back into another kind of world. Everything was different when you were alone. No more childhood pals. No mother or father, no teachers, and worst of all, no husband and lover.

She could have wept but didn't. She switched on the lights and went through to the kitchen to put the kettle on. She struggled to concentrate on her proposed visit to South Castle-on-Sea. Mr Webster would look after her well, and it would be interesting to meet his clever inventor and any wholesalers he had there. He had been dealing with others in South Castle-on-Sea before he'd had the good fortune to meet the inventor, and he still dealt with the others. The toy department catered for all tastes and ages. Mr Webster was one of the most trusted and able of her staff. She had always had faith in him and his abilities, and he had built up the department until it was the most successful financially, and in every other way, in the store.

She began to feel more positive and cheerful. Yes, she was really looking forward to her visit.

IO

'You're spoiling them, darling,' Moira said. Sam Webster went on handing out notes to each of his daughters.

'They work hard and deserve a bit of a reward now and again. Away and treat yourselves, girls.'

'Thanks, Daddy.' His daughters hugged and kissed him before hurrying off to examine all the windows of the Princes Square speciality and designer-label shops. They'd all enjoyed a good dinner in the downstairs courtyard and he and Moira had just been served with coffee.

They looked out on to a huge area with a brightly coloured floor and, overhead, was a clear glass roof. At one side stood a grand piano. Nobody was playing it at the moment but often there was a pianist there. People would lean from the upper galleries to look and listen. Sometimes there would be a group playing or a choir singing. The place had a great variety of restaurants as well as shops, and a wall of paintings and counters of silver and jewellery. You name it, Princes Square had it, and all at the luxury end of the market. To think that it had once been a dark, dirty lane with stables and offices and coach houses. Now even the outside on Buchanan Street was luxurious and impressive. Glass arched canopies contained within flowing wrought metalwork extended over the pavement. High on top of the building sat a huge silver peacock with its silver tail stretched wide, and hanging from the edge of the roof was a line of silver chandeliers.

Moira sighed. 'I wish you didn't need to keep going away down south. I hate it when you're away from home. It's not so bad when it's just somewhere in Scotland where you can get back the same day, or the next morning.'

'I hate it too, Moira, but it's the nature of the job.'

She sighed again. 'I know, but I can't help hating it at times.'

Oh, didn't he hate it at times too! The words 'away down south' immediately brought back all the worries and now horrors of South Castle-on-Sea. When Mrs Goodman announced she was coming with him, he had gone rigid with shock and horror. What on earth had possessed her – now of all times – to suddenly decide to go to South Castle-on-Sea? Things had been bad enough without her adding to the problem and complicating the situation even further. How on earth was he going to prevent her bumping into Viv? Or Viv seeing them? He could skulk around the back streets. Mrs Goodman would not. She would expect him to show her around all the best parts and Viv's B. & B. was in the best part, on the seafront, looking right onto the pier. Indeed, Mrs Goodman would wonder why he didn't book her in there. He had compromised by booking a couple of rooms in a good hotel on the seafront, but away at the other end from Viv's place.

He was still in an agony of anxiety and suspense. In the end, he decided it might be best to write to Viv or phone her and tell her that he was coming with his boss on his next visit. He would not be staying in her place because, as he'd already made plain, their relationship was over and he thought it wiser in the circumstances to make a booking elsewhere.

Otherwise, if Viv did bump into him with Mrs Goodman, she might think he'd got another woman and be enraged. There was no telling what Viv was capable of. Mrs Goodman was older than him, but she was a nice-looking woman with her blonde hair and shapely figure. She didn't look her age.

He phoned eventually and was much relieved to get Viv's answering machine. Better that than having to have any sort of conversation with her.

The few days at work passed almost in a dream. Or a nightmare, to be more accurate. Moira noticed and said worriedly, 'Sam, is there something wrong? You look so tense.'

'Oh, I suppose it's just the thought of the boss coming with me on this next trip. I'm not sure what her idea is. She says she just wants to meet the inventor but it feels as if she's going to be watching my every move.'

'I'm sure it'll be just as she says, darling. Why should she want to watch your every move? You're one of her most successful employees. She's never had any complaints about you, has she?'

'No.'

'Well, then.'

'It just doesn't seem right.'

Moira gave him a comforting kiss. 'Try to relax, Sam. Just do your job the same as usual. And it's only for a few days, after all.'

He nodded. But he couldn't relax. Who could, even if they had nothing to hide? Anybody would feel a bit tense and anxious with thoughts of the boss breathing down their neck from morning to night. Even just for a few days.

He even worried about Viv not getting the message he'd left on her answering machine. Often landladies went away in the winter. The summer was the busy time in all the seaside hotels and B. & B.s. In the winter, there was never much – if any – trade and so most landladies and hotel owners took a winter holiday abroad.

What if Viv had been away and didn't get his message, and then saw him with Mrs Goodman? Bad enough to see him at all, but to see him with an attractive woman . . . But now he was being ridiculous. He knew it. Even if she'd been abroad, or away anywhere, Viv would still get the message. The first thing most people did on their return was play back their answering machine messages.

She could still pester him, though, or do something to purposely cause trouble. He cursed the day he'd walked into her B. & B. From the moment he'd arrived at the reception desk, she was on to him. She gave him every 'come on' signal in the book. She even came out with corny things like, 'It's not often I get such a tall, dark and handsome man in here looking for a bed.'

He had smiled. Otherwise he'd tried to ignore her unexpected behaviour. This wasn't his normal reception in hotels. And anyway, he was tired after a long drive and just wanted a drink and to relax. He'd thought of Moira and the wonderfully relaxing atmosphere of their pretty little bungalow in respectable Bearsden. And he wished he was back there.

But there was no wishing a woman like Viv away. He had been flattered by her eager attention, of course, and he had succumbed to her charms. Idiot that he had been. He might have known that a woman like that was bound to cause trouble. Well, no use berating himself now. He'd just have to get on with it as best he could. After all, maybe Viv would accept his words as final and make no trouble at all. He couldn't convince himself and when it came to the actual day of the journey to South Castle-on-Sea, he was stiff with apprehension.

Mrs Goodman noticed. 'You're unusually quiet, Mr Webster.'

'Sorry, I've a lot on my mind at the moment.'

'Is there anything I can do to help?'

'No, it's personal stuff. But thanks all the same. Now, where would you like to stop for coffee?' He forced his voice to sound cheerful. 'I know a nice place in Gretna. Is that too long to wait?' He detailed a list of places he usually called at for coffee, lunch and afternoon tea.

Eventually Abi interrupted him. 'Mr Webster, you don't need to make conversation all the way to South Castle-on-Sea. I'd prefer it if you just concentrated on your driving.'

After that, he was thankfully silent, only exchanging a few pleasantries with her over coffee or a meal. The journey would have been fine if it hadn't been for all his worries about Viv.

Once in South Castle-on-Sea, he saw Abi safely to her room in the tall, many-storeyed hotel. It was very different from Viv's place. Viv's was called The Floral because of the ring of flowers surrounding it from early summer right through till autumn. Even in winter it had an attractive splash of colour with potted plants. It was small but had an excellent location on the most popular and busiest part of the front. This hotel was away at the far end in a quiet area.

Mrs Goodman had suggested a walk after she'd unpacked, and asked if he'd accompany her. He struggled to look perfectly happy to do so. Soon, however, she was saying, 'Why on earth are we going around all the quiet back streets?'

'There are some nice shops and boutiques I thought you'd like to see.'

'Most of them are shut.'

'True, but now you'll know where they are if you want to go out on your own tomorrow.'

'For goodness' sake, Mr Webster, I've just come from a shop. I want to walk along the front and enjoy the sea air and see all that's going on on the pier.'

'Of course.'

With a sinking heart, he changed direction. He began feverishly thinking and planning what he'd say and do if confronted by Viv. He kept praying that she was in Cyprus or Tenerife – anywhere but here. If she was here, however, and she was not outside, she could glance from one of her windows and see him. He cursed his six feet four. He could so easily be picked out in any crowd.

He steeled himself not to look over at The Floral as they reached it. He strolled on to the pier with Mrs Goodman at his side as if he were doing the most natural thing in the world.

II

Norman McKay was quaking inside but he was determined to go through with his plan. He had to now. He'd taken the plunge and booked Jenny into the clinic. Bills at the clinic were to be paid at the end of each month and the end of the month was not far away. He worked at the store as normal all day, although it seemed a miracle that he had managed to do so. Eventually, he collected several thousand pounds and, after he'd locked up as usual and with the money in his case, he left the shop by the back door. A narrow lane stretched along the back of the store. The back wall was of solid brick, with only a few lavatory windows at the very top. At one part, there was the back entrance. As well as stairs up to the departments, it had stairs going down to the basement, where dispatch was situated and the workshops of the electricians and joiners.

In an adjoining area just inside the door, two lines of bins were situated. There was never much rubbish to fill them, except perhaps some packaging materials, and dust from the cleaners' hoovers, and occasionally some food such as sandwiches from the canteen that had gone past their sell-by date. More often than not, however, the less fussy canteen workers would take the 'past their sell-by date' stuff home. That was allowed, although dates were always checked at the door just to make sure that there was no fiddling going on.

The bins were emptied once a week and the bins were put out in the back lane the night before the bin men came. They came early in the morning, after he arrived. He started work before eight o'clock and he always heard the arrival of the bin lorry around eight-thirty.

On this occasion, after all the staff had left, he locked up but instead of leaving from the front door, he left by the back. He had often done this before when going to the bank. It was one of a variety of ways and times that was part of his safety plan. The bins were sitting out in the lane, ready for the arrival of the bin men next morning. He placed the caseful of money into one of the bins. Carefully he covered it with some wood shavings and discarded sandwiches. Then he walked some way along the lane and drew a deep breath to gather every vestige of courage he had, before crashing his brow against the store wall. Blood poured down his face but he managed to stem it with a large handkerchief he had ready. Then, staggering slightly, he forced himself along the lane until he emerged at the other end and walked rather unsteadily along the road towards the bank.

It was quite a distance away but thankfully the streets were not busy. Most people who worked in the area were on their way home. Keeping his head down and the handkerchief against his brow, he eventually hailed a taxi and asked to be taken to the nearest hospital. There, at casualty, he told them he had been attacked outside the bank by two men and the money had been stolen. He asked them to call the police.

After they had done various tests and put a dressing and bandage on his head, he was interviewed by the police before being taken home.

The bank was quite a distance from the lane and so he was confident that the police would not see the need to search or make enquiries there. Their attention would be in the area around the bank, he felt sure. Once he'd retrieved the money early in the morning, before the bin men or anyone else arrived, his plan would be complete. The now urgent necessity to pay the money had given him the desperation he needed to carry out such a plan. But he wanted to get rid of the money right away so that Jenny would be safe and be sure of getting the full course of treatment. He had told her he had been saving and had also received a bonus from work and at last had enough to cover the treatment.

He lay on his bed, feeling lonely without her. His head throbbed painfully. At the same time, he felt thankful and relieved that he'd managed to gather enough courage to carry out the plan. Perhaps one day he would be able, somehow, to pay the money back. It was a terrible thing to cheat the store, and therefore to cheat Mrs Goodman. But he'd had no choice. It had to be done.

After a restless night, he got up earlier than usual and hurried to the store. There he wasted no time in going to the bin to retrieve the money.

It wasn't there.

He was so shocked he couldn't move at first. Then he scrabbled among the sandwiches and paper and wood shavings. Still nothing. He tried the other bins in case he'd made a mistake about which bin he'd put the money in. But he knew he had not made a mistake. He was sweating now and trembling. He couldn't understand it. The only thought that came to him was that some tramp must have come looking for food or something out of the bins. He should have thought of that, but never, in all his years at the store, had he seen or heard of any tramp in the area. Could it be that the police had searched here after all and they had found the money? But it couldn't have been that. They would have let him know immediately.

Shock, fear, tears of disappointment and disbelief turned to fury. Whoever had done this – he'd find them and kill them. The money could have saved Jenny's life. The doctor had warned him right from the start that she only had a few months left at the very most. It could be weeks, or even days. Alone in the dark, silent lane, he wept again. Then he heard the bin lorry in the distance. The bin men would soon be in the lane. With an effort, he forced himself back into the store. What was he going to do? He couldn't get away with staging another robbery. He would have to think of something else. But at the same time, his fury at someone taking the money, denying Jenny her immediate chance of life, overruled everything else. If it meant trawling the streets of Glasgow every hour of every night, he'd find the bastard. He'd find him. He'd get the money back or whatever of it was left. And he'd kill the bastard. He'd kill him.

Somehow he managed to work as usual – well, almost as usual – that day. Everyone was sympathetic, of course, and said he should not be in at work at all with his head injury and with being so upset. He should be at home resting and recovering from such a shock. Then whispers behind his back of 'Such a conscientious, hard-working man'. It made him feel ashamed. If they only knew what he'd done. He kept to his office most of the day and attended to phone calls and paperwork as best he could. He had promised Jenny he would go to the clinic to see her after work and so, once he'd had a cup of tea and had taken a couple of painkillers, he locked up and made his way to the clinic.

He knew something had happened the moment he set foot in the place. The doctor's serious face told him all he feared before a word was spoken. Jenny had died only half an hour previously. A dreadful thought struck him. Maybe the physical effort and all the worry of being moved from her own bed and across the city had been too much for her. That had been his

12

Before leaving for South Castle-on-Sea, Abi had gone to Edinburgh. It had been dry but cold. That was usually the way of it. Edinburgh had a cold east wind that probably kept the rain at bay most days. Glasgow was warmer, but wetter. Abi got off the train at Waverley Station and began walking towards the High Street. She wanted to tell John of her plan to visit South Castle-on-Sea. She could have told him over the phone that she was going down south for a few days, but she wanted to see him before leaving. Sometimes she took a taxi from the station but this time she felt like a walk. Also, she wanted to stock up with food from the gourmet food shops near the Royal Mile. The shops there sold delicious smoked salmon, kippers, a great variety of cheeses, not to mention haggis, oatcakes, shortbread and Dundee cake.

She was a traditionalist. She not only preferred traditional Scottish food, she even preferred the Old Town to the Georgian New Town. The Royal Mile in the Old Town had at one time been the hub of the city. All Edinburgh life revolved around this single street. It ran from Edinburgh Castle sitting on top of Castle Rock, an ancient volcano, right down to the Palace of Holyroodhouse and Holyrood Abbey. It was in fact a succession of four streets – Castle Hill, the Lawnmarket, the High Street and the Canongate – with scores of narrow side streets or closes jutting out like ribs on either side.

Abi passed John Knox's house and remembered something she'd read about him meeting with the young Mary, Queen of Scots. Mary had not long arrived from France, where she'd had an elegant upbringing in the Royal Court. She said to Knox that she wanted the people of Scotland to continue to worship freely in the way they had always done, as long as she could worship in her own way. But John Knox would have none of it. Stubborn, bigoted old so-and-so, Abi thought.

Here she was again outside the Scottish Parliament, and again feeling a bit confused once through the entrance. Security was a nuisance, but she supposed in today's world it was a necessity. She obediently emptied her handbag and pockets and went through, on this occasion without a ping or the need to be frisked. She was getting used to the lack of directions, and made for the next counter in the main area, where she was given an identity card to hang around her neck. She told them about John, and a girl at the desk phoned him and then told her to go and have a cup of tea and he'd be down in half an hour or so because he was in the middle of something.

But first of all she went over to the shop and bought some special sweets for the children. Then she wandered round to have a look at Queensberry House, which was now attached, incongruously, to the Parliament building. It had been built as far back as 1667 and had been the home of the second Duke of Queensberry at the time of the signing of the Treaty of Union in 1707. For a time, it had been used as a public hospital, then as an army barracks, then as a 'House of Refuge'. Eventually it had been bought by Scottish & Newcastle Breweries, who owned the rest of the surrounding site at the time. Now it provided office accommodation for the Presiding Officers and other parliamentary staff. There was also a room in it called the Dewar Room, which housed a collection of books and other memorabilia that had belonged to Donald Dewar, Scotland's first First Minister. He had died before the Parliament building had been completed. The architect, Enric Miralles, had also died and had never seen the work completed. Abi had heard that politicians had subsequently interfered with the design and the builders had kept upping their price as a result.

Many people complained about the cost of the Parliament but John had quoted various buildings in England, especially in London, that had cost as much, and often very much more.

'For instance, the refurbishment of the Ministry of Defence headquarters in London cost two point three billion. Nobody made any fuss about that, did they?' he said.

John had been surprised but pleased when she told him her news about going down to South Castle-on-Sea. 'Och well, the change will do you good. Get plenty of good sea air into those lungs of yours.'

Then of course, once in South Castle-on-Sea, Mr Webster had behaved a bit oddly at first and taken her round the back streets of the place to see shops. Shops! What on earth was he thinking of? Of course, he had told her that he had a lot on his mind. She wondered if there was trouble at home, though she'd met Mrs Webster, who seemed a lovely woman who adored her husband. He seemed to adore her too and he was very proud of his daughters.

However, she did eventually get a walk along the seafront. It did her good and she felt relaxed and ready for a good dinner. It was a pity that Mr Webster had booked her into a hotel so far away from the centre. Why not that lovely little place directly opposite the pier with the potted plants all around it? It would have been so interesting watching from those windows all that was going on, all the entertainment on the pier.

She would never have expected Mr Webster to disappoint her like this. The only excuse she could think of was that his mind was not on what he was doing. Admittedly, the hotel was comfortable and it was fascinating to meet the old gentleman who invented all the wonderful toys they stocked in the toy department. But after quite a long visit, she refused Mr Webster's suggestion to go back to the hotel for lunch. Instead, she insisted on another walk along the promenade.

'Why don't we try that pretty place opposite the pier?' she suggested. She was taken aback by the look of horror that spread over Mr Webster's face. It was only for a couple of seconds, but there was no mistaking the immediate reflex of horror.

'Oh, no,' he said, apparently recovering his composure but avoiding her eyes. 'They don't do luncheon. It's just a B. & B. place.'

He was hiding something. That was it. The obvious answer was a woman. She wasn't daft. He was having it off with another woman. He was secretly being unfaithful to his wife. No wonder he was shocked when she announced she was coming with him to South Castle-on-Sea. He didn't want to be found out. She was shocked herself now. It was the last thing she would have expected of Mr Webster. Some of the other buyers, yes. But not Mr Webster. He had everything going for him – a lovely and loving wife, two attractive daughters. The more she thought about what he was doing to his wife and family, the more angry she became. She wanted to sack him right there and then. She struggled to control the impulse. Strictly speaking, it was not a sacking offence. It was his own private life and it was not affecting his job. Another thought struck her. If she did sack him, it might very well affect the toy department. Could he, would he, take his agreement with the old toy inventor elsewhere? Any of the big stores in Glasgow or elsewhere would jump at the chance of a contract like that and a buyer like Mr Webster. To sack Mr Webster would be hurting Goodmans, not him.

She was stiffly quiet all the journey home and gave him only a brief, polite thank-you when they parked outside her house. She didn't even ask him in for a cup of tea, even though she would have been glad of some company – any company. The house was always coldly silent. You could almost touch the silence, it was so heavy and strong.

She switched on the television. It was one of the soaps and the characters all seemed so unreal, some storylines stretching out for so long that she had become fed up with them. She put the kettle on, then returned to the sitting room to fiddle with the programme controls. There was an antiques programme, a cooking programme, and something about wildlife; none of them awakened any interest in her.

Her eyes kept straying over to the window and the rustling, swaying trees. Tom used to love looking out at the garden. In the summer they both enjoyed sitting outside. Sometimes they had a barbecue. Tom always took charge of that. Outside and inside, everything and everywhere had been lovely when he had been there. Now the sights and sounds outside only served to increase her loneliness and despair, and even pepper her with fear and apprehension. She could not resist going over and jerking shut the heavy curtains. Clinging on to them, she leaned her head against the cool material.

Mr Webster did not know how lucky he was to have his loving partner. Obviously, he did not appreciate his good fortune. Life was so unfair. Her anger at Mr Webster returned. She nursed it through to the kitchen and the intensity of it made her hand tremble as she made herself a cup of tea. His behaviour was despicable and he didn't deserve to get away with it.

She wondered if she should have a straight talk with him, tell him what she thought of his behaviour. For a minute, though, it occurred to her that it might all be in her imagination. But no, the signs were all there. He looked, acted, and was as guilty as hell.

She felt almost unbearably restless and only one of her *CSI: Miami* DVDs managed to capture her attention. Only Horatio's gentleness, his quiet, caring personality, soothed her chaotic emotions. She relaxed back into the cushions of the chair. Dear Horatio was so like Tom.

13

It was hard to believe, Miss Eden thought, as she gazed from her window, that Springburn had once been a hamlet inhabited by weavers, quarry workers and farm hands. The opening of the Edinburgh and Glasgow Railway changed all that. Soon Springburn became as famed for building locomotives as Govan had been for ships. When heavy engineering went into decline, the Corporation of Glasgow started to implement their urban renewal policy. This mainly meant new roadways, which destroyed eighty per cent of the old tenements and caused them to disappear under rubble. They were replaced by deck-access housing and high-rise flats, completely extinguishing the close friendships and community spirit of the past.

Miss Eden missed all the old shops, especially the Co-op, whose proud boast was that they looked after everyone from the cradle to the grave. All the old landmarks had gone. Now it was all motorways. The graveyard was still there but the New Kinema picture house had long since disappeared. It had been known as 'The Coffin' because of its shape and the fact that it was over the wall from Sighthill Cemetery.

Miss Eden sighed. She did not usually have this longing for the far-distant past of her childhood. She reckoned it must simply be a sign of feeling insecure in the present. The past seemed safer.

She'd had a reply to her advert. A meeting had been arranged for the next day. The man, Andreas Palchinskaite, was Lithuanian. He was lonely, his reply had explained, and he wanted to meet a good Scottish woman with a view to 'forming a serious relationship'. Did that mean marriage? She had heard that foreign women married Scottish men in order to get a British passport and British citizenship. However, there had been plenty of foreign men who were equally guilty of this.

Was that was Andreas was after? Or was this just a case of her suspicious detective mind at work again? She decided it would do no harm at least to meet him. She needn't commit herself to anything. To be on the safe side, she suggested a lunchtime meeting instead of an evening one. She chose a place near Goodmans, so that she would have an excuse to leave him and make an easy return to work. She felt in a strange mood, which lasted all evening and into the next day. Was it a kind of intuition? She very nearly didn't go to The Granary, the nearby healthfood shop with a few tables in an open area for everyone to see. There should be nothing to worry about there. And yet, she hesitated up to the last moment. Pulling herself together, she left Goodmans and walked along Glassford Street.

There was only one male customer in the shop. He was sitting at a table behind a block of shelving, not at the tables by the window. Hiding? she wondered, but firmly put the idea out of her mind. She was becoming really paranoid. She approached him saying, 'Andreas?'

He rose immediately, clicking his heels and bowing over her outstretched hand.

'It is a pleasure to meet you, Miss Eden.' He indicated a seat. 'You didn't tell me your first name. May I ask what it is?'

'Doris.'

'What an attractive name.'

That was a lie for a start. She had always hated her name and was grateful that only second names were used in Goodmans.

The young waitress came over then and they ordered the home-made soup, a mixed salad and crusty bread, followed by coffee. Andreas told her he was a nurse in an old people's care home. She was aware that there were many male nurses nowadays but it surprised her that he should be one. He looked more like a heavyweight boxer: broad-shouldered, strong-jawed, with piercing blue eyes. She had imagined and hoped for a more refined, sensitive type of man. Perhaps a writer or an artist, somebody creative. If he was a nurse, though, he must have some sensitivity and caring in his nature, especially working in a care home for the elderly. He asked about her job and she told him she was an assistant in a family department store.

She began to warm to him as he told her more about his job and how important he felt it was to look after people with age-related problems. He did his best for the old people, he said, but he couldn't help feeling depressed at times by their plight.

'It comes to all of us eventually, Doris, and it is a depressing thought. Especially if one comes home every night with nothing to distract one's thoughts. I watch television but that is living an artificial life and a lonely one, don't you think?'

She agreed and admitted that she felt something similar. They felt exactly the same about lots of things as it turned out, and it was good to be able to talk to someone who understood. Soon it was as if they had known each other for years, they were talking so freely and earnestly together. The pretty girl assistant asked them if they'd like more coffee and it came as a sudden surprise to realise that there was someone else present. It had been as if they were away in a world of their own.

They finished their coffee and he asked, 'When can I see you again, Doris?'

'Do you work shifts?'

'Yes, and I am working evenings this week, but I could see you at lunchtime again tomorrow. Then next week, if you agree, we could have dinner together. I will be on early shift next week and so free every evening.'

She smiled and rose. 'Until tomorrow then? But I must rush back to work now.'

He pulled her hand to his lips. 'I shall look forward to seeing you again. It has been such a pleasure.'

As she passed the window outside, she glanced in and saw him standing at the counter waiting to pay the bill. He was really a fine figure of a man. It was perfectly appropriate that he should have such a muscular figure. No doubt his job entailed having to be able to lift heavy patients. He was a handsome, caring, hard-working man.

What more could she want? She returned to Goodmans with a spring in her step. Little fountains of happiness and excitement kept bubbling to the surface. Her efforts to calm herself and tell herself she was being childish and stupid were all to no avail.

She blessed the day she'd put the advert in the paper. Of course, she had no intention of mentioning it to anyone. She knew the reaction she would get – all the cautions and warnings she'd already given herself. Now she didn't care. Even after that one meeting, she felt they were soulmates.

In the afternoon, it was quite a struggle to concentrate on her job. The first person she had to deal with was an alcoholic woman who lived in a homeless place – a real dump where they put everyone out in the morning to walk the streets until it was bedtime again. This woman had come from a well-off family and she was obviously well educated. However, because of the drink, her family had disowned her. She carried all her worldly possessions in a large handbag she always clutched close to her. Every shop in the area knew her. Rather than have to go back to the homeless people's place, she preferred to get arrested and spend some time in a police station or in prison.

'Come on, Marion,' Miss Eden said, 'give me the watch.'

'What watch?' Marion slurred.

'I saw you.'

'I'm away.' She lurched towards the door.

Miss Eden sighed and followed the frowsy-haired woman outside. The security guard stepped outside with them.

'All right, I have reason to believe . . .' Miss Eden began her usual spiel and the woman staggered back inside the store with her and upstairs to the manager's office.

Miss Eden felt sorry for the manager. She had thought there was something bothering him and it turned out his wife had been ill. Then, as if it wasn't enough to be mugged and robbed, his wife had died.

He had been encouraged to take more time off but said he'd go mad if he had to spend all day and every day in the house on his own. So would she. It was bad enough every evening and at weekends. But now her luck had changed.

That evening she had a bath and washed her hair and sat smiling to herself as she wielded her hair dryer. She had something to look forward to now. What a difference it made to life. It gave it that little extra personal dimension. Before, it had been all work and very little play. Only her karate, and even that was work-connected. She had to be strong and fit and quick off the mark for her job. She had to be able to defend herself.

Oh, how glad she was that she'd put the advert in the paper. She couldn't concentrate on the television. She kept seeing in her mind's eye the strong face of Andreas. He hadn't been in Scotland very long, apparently, but liked the country. He especially liked Glasgow. People were friendly and made him feel at home. Nevertheless, he was shy at forming relationships and had got into the habit of just returning to his lodgings after work. It was not enjoyable to go out on one's own, he said. She agreed. She knew exactly what he meant and how he felt.

The next day, lunchtime seemed an eternity in coming. Even though she had been kept busy as usual, time still didn't pass quickly enough. She had to do a bit of staff training. For one thing, she had to make sure all the staff knew what to do in order to control their fitting rooms. They had also to keep the display windows locked during the day. Recently a lock on the window displaying dummies wearing expensive designer-label coats had been picked and the coats stolen. This was during the day and she had been off duty.

'During the day?' she'd said unbelievingly to the manager. 'And all the dummies were in the window?'

'No,' Mr McKay had said. 'All the dummies were on the shop floor because the staff never saw anyone going in.'

After the staff training session, she received a message on her mobile asking her to go urgently to the children's department on the first floor. There was a woman with a baby in a pram . . . That was always worth watching. It was the same with shopping trolleys. They could be perfectly innocent, of course, but so often stolen goods were taken out hidden in prams or shopping trolleys.

What with making arrests and filling out reports, she began to fear she would be too late for lunch. Indeed, she was ten minutes late and was panicking as she hurried along Glassford Street. She was at least thankful that she had agreed to the meeting in The Granary again. It was only minutes from Goodmans. What a blessed relief it was to see him sitting at one of the tables near the window this time. She smiled and waved at him and he smiled and waved back.

'I'm sorry I'm late,' she announced breathlessly when she reached him.

He stood and gave her his little bow. 'You are here. That is all that matters.'

Yes, that was all that mattered. She was here with him.

14

'Is that you, Sam?'

He nearly dropped his mobile. He was sitting in one of the morning meetings in Mrs Goodman's office surrounded by other buyers and managerial staff. Not to mention Douglas and Minna Benson.

'I'm in the middle of an important meeting,' he managed. 'Could you please call back later?'

Then he apologised to Mrs Goodman and switched the mobile off.

It was Viv on the phone. God knows what she was going to say. Or even where she was calling from. Please God it's not from Glasgow, he fervently thought. He hardly heard what was said or decided at the meeting, he was so worried about the call.

It was lunchtime when she called again.

'What is it you want?' His voice sounded harder, harsher, than he'd meant it to.

'Don't you dare talk to me like that.'

'But, Viv . . .' He struggled to modify his tone and make it seem more reasonable. 'I thought I'd already made myself perfectly clear. There's nothing more to be said.'

'Oh, I've a lot more to say to you, Sam.'

'Viv, we're finished. We never really got started, in fact. What we had was little more than a one-night stand. It didn't mean anything.'

'You think not? Well, you could have fooled me. In fact, you obviously did fool me. Well, you're not going to get away with it. Believe me, Sam Webster, you haven't heard the last of this.'

And she hung up.

He groaned inside. What the hell was she going to do? His greatest fear was that she would come up to Glasgow and somehow confront his wife and family. He wondered if it would do any good if he went down to South Castle-on-Sea and faced her, had it out with her once and for all. Maybe he should try that. Should he phone her first and tell her he was coming down? If he was going to confront her, he'd better do it right away, in case she was on the point of leaving South Castle-on-Sea and arriving in Glasgow any day now – tomorrow, even.

He couldn't bear to do nothing, just to wait. He called her back.

'Viv, I'm coming down to South Castle-on-Sea tomorrow. I'll leave first thing in the morning and come and see you as soon as I arrive. All right?'

'OK by me.'

'See you tomorrow then.'

'OK.'

It was a relief in a way that he'd managed to contact her and make this arrangement. It meant she wouldn't be rushing up to Glasgow. Hopefully, this time, he would manage – somehow – to make her see sense and accept the inevitable.

He went home early and took Moira a bouquet of flowers. One of his daughters had gone back to Edinburgh University. The other was as usual attending Glasgow University, but tonight she was out clubbing with some friends.

'Oh, how lovely, Sam. Thank you, darling.' Moira took the flowers and went through to the kitchen with them. 'I'll stand them in the basin until after we've had our meal. Then I'll arrange them in a vase.' She laughed. 'I'll probably need two vases. You're far too good to me, Sam.'

He kissed the top of her head and put his arms around her waist.

'I'm not good enough for you,' he muttered, and he meant it.

She twisted round to face him and gazed up at him. 'Darling, how can you say such a thing? You've always been a good husband, and lover, and father. What more could any woman possibly want?'

Loyalty? Faithfulness?, he thought. He had always tried to be a good husband, right enough. But there had been the occasional lapse and now one of them was catching up with him.

'It's a damn nuisance,' he said, 'but I've got to go back down to South Castle-on-Sea tomorrow. But it'll just be for one night. I might even be able to get back in the same day, if I leave early enough.'

'No, no, darling, that would be too stressful for you. Stay the night.'

'Are you sure you won't mind?'

'Of course not. It's your job.'

Sometimes he wished she wouldn't be so reasonable and sympathetic. It made him feel even more guilty.

He left earlier than usual the next day. He wanted to get the ordeal he faced with Viv over and done with as soon and as quickly as possible. He had already booked in to a B. & B. near the centre of the town. No way was he going to stay overnight with Viv. What he should have done in the first place was walk out the moment she came on to him. That was when he should have booked in at the other B. & B. Any other B. & B. Oh, how he wished he had.

She was waiting for him, standing at the window, peering

out. As soon as he stepped inside, she tried to embrace him. He pushed her away.

'For God's sake, Viv, how many times must I tell you! There's nothing between us. Nothing at all. It was as you said at the beginning – we were both lonely. I was away from home and missing my wife and family. As a result of that terrible period of loneliness, I was unfaithful to my wife a few times with you. That is something I bitterly regret.'

'All right, Sam.' Her tone became soft and wheedling. 'You don't need to leave your wife but what's wrong with going on as we were? Keeping each other company and enjoying each other while you're here?'

'Viv, I've booked into another place for tonight and I intend staying there every time I'm in South Castle-on-Sea after this. I should not have slept with you, or anyone else, and I'm sorry. It's certainly never going to happen again.'

'You smug, hypocritical pig! Don't you go all goody-goody on me. You can't just brush me off whenever you feel like it.'

'Viv, calm down. What's the point of suddenly getting all worked up about this? I was perfectly straight with you right from the beginning. I told you my wife was the only one I cared about and you said you understood, but there was no harm in us having a bit of fun occasionally and enjoying each other's company when I was in South Castle-on-Sea. Those were your very words.'

'Oh, so it's all my fault, is it?'

'I'm not saying that. If it's anyone's fault, it's mine. And I repeat – I'm sorry, but whatever it was, and whoever's fault it was, it doesn't matter now because it's over. I'm going now, Viv, and I don't want to hear from you again. So please don't write to me or phone me or contact me in any way again, because it won't change anything.'

'Oh, won't it? We'll soon see about that.'

'What do you mean?'

'Your wife might think of changing something if she gets to know that you were having an affair.'

'I have not been having an affair.'

'And once she knows about this little affair, she'll begin to wonder how many other affairs there've been. One in every place you visit?'

'You're mad. What's the point in all this? What do you think you'll gain by it?'

'Satisfaction, Sam. The satisfaction that you won't be getting away with just dumping me when the fancy takes you.'

'You're a malicious, vindictive, stupid woman, and I'm warning you, if you hurt my wife in any way, you'll regret it. I'll see to that.'

'Oh, I'm quaking in my shoes, big man,' she sneered.

He strode away from the house and out onto the promenade. He was glad of the cold wind blowing from the sea. It helped cool his anger. It did not, however, relax the tight pain in his head. With his fists bunched into his coat pockets, he hurried along the promenade and round a corner towards the B. & B. he had booked into. All the time, he was feverishly trying to think what he could do. Should he phone Moira and give her some sort of warning? Viv could phone her tonight. Or would she wait and travel up to Glasgow, and actually go and see Moira? It was an appalling vision.

There was a pub near the B. & B. and he went in and ordered a double whisky. It didn't help. He had another and that did nothing to help him either. He bought a half bottle and took it up to his room. It didn't change anything or go any way to solve the problem, but at least it knocked him out eventually and he didn't regain consciousness until nearly nine o'clock the next morning. He dressed hurriedly and took a quick breakfast before setting off in his car for Glasgow. He couldn't concentrate on doing any business. That would have to wait until his next visit. All he wanted to do was to get home as quickly as possible. He didn't know what he was going to do there, but he had to do something.

He wondered if he should confess to Moira. Get his word in first. The mere thought made him feel sick. It took all his will-power to concentrate on his driving. But he couldn't help thinking, 'What a mess!'

And he kept remembering how lucky he had been with such a lovely wife and children and such a happy home. Viv was going to do her damnedest to ruin it all. No doubt she would put on a great act as the poor, hard-done-by, deceived and abandoned woman.

There was nothing else for it. He would have to confess the truth to Moira. He prayed that he would get to her first.

15

Mr McKay started his search in the Merchant City area – first of all in the streets and lanes nearest to Glassford Street. On the corner of Glassford Street and Argyle Street was Marks & Spencer's, and there was a plaque on the shop wall at the corner of Argyle Street and Virginia Street. It was where the Black Bull Inn had been. Robert Burns stayed there when he wrote to Agnes McLehose. She didn't want their correspondence to be known and suggested they sign their letters 'Sylvander' and 'Clarinda'. Before she died, Agnes wrote in her journal, 'I parted with Burns in the year 1791, never more to meet in this world, may we meet in heaven.'

Oh, how Mr McKay echoed those words – broken-heartedly. And the words of the poem Burns wrote to his 'Clarinda' – 'Ae Fond Kiss'.

> Ae fond kiss, and then we sever;
> Ae fareweel, and then forever! . . .
> Had we never lov'd sae blindly,
> Never met – or never parted,
> We had ne'er been broken-hearted.

He wandered around wearing something he'd bought earlier that day – a dark, hooded anorak, with the hood pulled well over his face. At the end of Ingram Street he came to the Gallery of Modern Art, in Queen Street. Even at this late hour, and despite the dark smir of rain, there were people squatting between the pillars and on the front steps. They were young people, some of them drinking out of cans and bottles, and laughing and fooling about. He didn't think any of them were tramps likely to be rooting in bins for something to eat.

The Gallery of Modern Art had been built originally as a tobacco lord's mansion house and in front of it was a statue of the Duke of Wellington on a horse. It had become a habit of the young people to climb up to the statue and put a traffic cone on the Duke of Wellington's head. Now even in Glasgow guide books, the picture of the Duke always showed him with the incongruous and undignified red and white traffic cone perched on his head.

Jenny used to laugh at that and say it was such a typically Glasgow thing to do. Jenny had a good sense of humour and she liked art. He had never understood, and certainly didn't appreciate much of the modern art in the gallery, but Jenny had.

He skulked into every corner and lane in Queen Street, until he reached Argyle Street, and then walked along Argyle Street and down every close, lane and alleyway until he reached the Trongate. Jenny had always been interested in the history of Glasgow and after she was confined to bed she spent a lot of her time reading books about the origins of the city. She had been particularly fascinated by this area. (Oh, how interested and full of life she had been. What a cruel waste!) Just west of King Street was the oldest music hall in the United Kingdom, the British Panopticon. Sixteen-year-old Stan Laurel had started here. There were mermaids and bearded ladies in the attic and a zoo in the basement with a Himalayan bear which escaped into the Trongate and terrorised everyone until it was shot by its eccentric owner, A. E. Pickard.

There was a dark area behind King Street where he saw a group of shadowy figures. Cautiously he approached them. They looked as if they were half unconscious with either drink or drugs, or both.

'I'm looking for a friend,' Mr McKay said. 'He came into a bit of money recently. Do you know him? Have you heard of anybody like that?'

There was a shaking of heads and mutters of 'Naw' and 'Sorry, son.'

He moved on down the lane to where another few men were squatting and drinking from a bottle of Buckfast tonic wine. He got no response from them at all.

Back on King Street he hesitated, not sure which way to turn. It could be that the man he was searching for was no longer on the streets, but living it up in a hotel. His only hope, he reckoned, was finding one or more people who knew, or had even heard about the change of fortune, the sudden acquisition of money, by one of their number. But the homeless tramps he'd come across so far were suspicious of him and obviously saw him as not one of them.

The rain became colder and heavier and he hugged his anorak tighter around his body. He was exhausted and miserable. Yet being at home for long empty evenings made him feel worse. His thoughts about Jenny became unbearably painful. And thoughts about the money and the man who'd stolen it. To think of anything was better than suffering desolation and guilt. Finding this man gave him something to concentrate on, gave him a purpose to live for.

He went along as far as the Tolbooth, on its island in the middle of the traffic. It was all that had survived of a much larger building that had once housed the courts and prison. People were chained to the walls here and prisoners' ears were nailed to the Tolbooth door. Further along, in the Gallowgate, there had been public hangings and nothing was better attended. The last hanging attracted over 100,000 people. How he would have enjoyed seeing the bastard who stole the money hanged. But hanging would be too good for him.

Where to go now? He stood across from the Tolbooth hunched into his wet anorak, his glasses blurring with rain. Should he go up the High Street or along the Saltmarket? Jenny had told him that the Saltmarket had been the place where middle-class burgesses of the town had houses fronting on to the main streets. Booths, or early shops, were situated in the lower halves of the houses, with the living accommodation above. Along the narrow vennels and wynds were other buildings which housed the craftsmen of the town – tanners, skinners, fullers, weavers, fleshers. The candlemakers moved to what was now known as Candleriggs. They were blamed for causing several great fires in the town. At one time, a third of the town had been destroyed by one of these fires and over a thousand families had been made homeless.

He kept thinking of Jenny's face, bright with interest and enthusiasm as she spoke about Glasgow's history. Often they'd come here on their way to Glasgow Green and when they reached the ancient green, she'd say, 'This is the site of a thousand battles, Norman. Can't you just feel the atmosphere?'

He couldn't but always hugged her arm, enjoying her enthusiasm.

'Battles here were fought by the people. The battles for "one man one vote", "one woman one vote", "a fair day's pay for a fair day's work", to mention just a few. Then there's the fairs, festivals, all sorts of entertainments and sport. This is the heart and soul of the social history of Glasgow, Norman.'

All he had known it as was the original home of both Celtic and Rangers football clubs. His only other interest in history was contained in the Trades Hall and Merchants House. He had always had a serious interest in his job and how trade had developed. He had worked up from the bottom to being manager and he had always been proud of how hard-working and conscientious he had been. And how meticulously honest. Until now.

If the money had still been there, he would have returned it to the shop. It was no use to him after Jenny had died. But he had been prevented from doing that by some stupid thieving bastard who'd probably never done a hard day's work in his life.

Fury quickened his steps and before he knew it, he was at the entrance of Glasgow Green. He couldn't bear even to look at the place, and shrunk away from it. Soon, he was passing the area where Oliver Cromwell had stayed while in Scotland. A minister called Boyd had verbally attacked Cromwell from the pulpit at a sermon Cromwell attended. The minister's hatred of Cromwell infuriated Cromwell's secretary, who told Cromwell that he should have the man beheaded. Cromwell declined and instead invited the minister to dinner. Jenny had always liked that story. She was a forgiving person. She had never even shown any bitterness at having to suffer her terrible illness and imminent death.

He had.

She was a Christian but he had lost whatever faith he once had. What kind of God was it – if there was a God – who could allow a beautiful, loving woman like Jenny to suffer so much?

Somehow, he got back to Argyle Street. He cursed the rain. No doubt most of the tramps were sheltering inside hostels for the homeless and the like, not hunkering about in lanes getting soaked. His whole evening had been a waste of time. He could have wept.

On the way home, he went into an off-licence and bought a bottle of whisky. He managed to drink a third of it before he reached the isolated villa on the outskirts of Bishopbriggs. He dreaded the ordeal of returning to the house and all the memories it contained. The drink knocked him out before he reached the bed upstairs and he awoke next day on the sitting room settee. He was still dressed, except for his soaking wet anorak, which, thank goodness, he'd managed to discard before collapsing unconscious.

Hurriedly, he washed and changed into clean clothes. He didn't wait to eat anything or even drink a cup of tea before leaving for work. He couldn't stay in the house a moment longer than was necessary. Only with a struggle did he manage to resist the temptation to swallow down a mouthful of whisky.

On arrival at the shop, he went through his usual routine, hoping that no one would see any difference in him, or suspect any difference. His only worry on that score was Miss Eden, with her usual piercing stare. At last he had time to go up to the canteen for a cup of hot, reviving tea. He didn't feel he could face any food but forced himself to eat a piece of toast. Then he had Mrs Goodman's morning meeting to cope with. His head was thumping and his mouth had gone dry again. Somehow, he got through the meeting. The buyers seemed to be taking up most of Mrs Goodman's attention, instead of the managers, this morning. He returned to his office to attend to phone calls, before making his routine inspection of the departments. All the time, he longed for a drink. He needed to drink himself into oblivion again.

Now not only thoughts of Jenny returned, but thoughts of the thief who'd taken the money began to obsess him. He had tried all that he could think of by searching around the lanes and closes and back streets. What else could he do?

'Are you all right, Mr McKay?' Miss Eden's voice jerked him back to his present surroundings.

He shook his head. 'I'm finding it difficult to cope. My poor wife, you know . . .'

'Yes, we are all so sorry, Mr McKay. If you ask me, you really need to take some time off to recover. I'm sure Mrs

Goodman would agree. There's no need in your present circumstances to struggle in to work every day. Why don't you speak to her?'

Nothing would help. It would only mean longer hours alone in the villa. But he nodded. 'Maybe I will. We'll see. Thank you for your concern, Miss Eden.'

He did not ask for any time off and had no intention of doing so. Just the thought of having nothing to do all day was a nightmare. His only comfort was alcohol. So far, he had at least managed to refrain from drinking while he was at work. Every evening, on the way home, however, he would go into a pub and drink himself practically unconscious. Eventually, a thought occurred to him – something that could help him in two ways. He'd have company and at the same time, he might be able to find the thief.

He remembered the homeless people he'd seen, groups of shabbily clothed men. He could buy some shabby clothes from Paddy's Market and join them. Probably the reason nobody spoke to him before was because he didn't look like one of them. This way he would get to know them. Then he might, in time, get to know the thief. The chances were that a man like that had already squandered the money on drink and drugs and would be back on the streets again. Or somebody would know something about him.

Paddy's Market was situated along the Bridgegate where a railway bridge crossed overhead. At this point, the narrow Shipbank Lane led to a flea market, as Paddy's Market was sometimes called. It was started in the nineteenth century by Irish immigrants, when it sold second-hand clothes to poor people who lived in nearby hovels. The traders sold their wares on the pavement and still did to this day. They had been offered decent premises but had refused, preferring to sell their second-hand goods in the traditional way.

Mr McKay picked his way gingerly between the coats,

jackets, dresses, trousers, skirts and other garments spread out on the pavement. He bought a pair of shabby brown trousers, a green and white striped collarless shirt, a navy waistcoat, a jersey, a dirty-looking raincoat, and a woollen hat. At the last minute he decided on a down-at-heel pair of shoes that were his size. His own shoes would look suspiciously good quality. He had bought them in the shoe department at Goodmans. Everything in Goodmans was of the highest quality. Before returning home, he went into an off-licence and bought a couple of bottles of Buckfast.

Later that night, he discarded his smart coat, his business suit, shirt and tie and polished shoes and dressed in everything he had bought at Paddy's Market. Then, under cover of darkness and with one of the bottles of Buckfast wine in his pocket, he made his way back into town.

16

The police had received a phone message telling them that a bomb had been planted in Goodmans of Glassford Street and a call had immediately come from the police to the store. The bomb had been set to go off within the hour and blow the whole place up. The store had to be evacuated immediately. This was a dreadfully difficult and complicated thing to do.

Miss Eden found herself having to take charge and do most of the organising. Mr McKay was confused and, to put it bluntly, completely useless. This was so unlike him. Mr McKay had always been calm, clear-headed and competent in any emergency. Of course, Miss Eden thought, the poor man was not himself just now. He should have taken her advice, spoken to Mrs Goodman, and got a spell off work to give him some time to recover.

'Will everyone please leave the building immediately,' she repeated over the intercom. 'Everyone gather outside in the street as quickly as possible.'

She went around the departments shooing everyone away as calmly as she could. It was difficult enough accomplishing this feat because of all the customers in the store, plus the staff. An extra worry was the opportunity for theft while all this was going on and her attention was diverted from her normal detective duties.

It was understandable in these harrowing circumstances that she completely forgot about her lunch date with Andreas. She had reached the ground floor and was shepherding the last of the staff outside when she spotted him. He was at the front of a mass of people now filling Glassford Street. The crowd were also spilling over into Wilson Street, Argyle Street and Ingram Street.

The police were also in Glassford Street now, and in the store with sniffer dogs. A couple of officers spoke to her and asked about the situation upstairs and in the offices and staff area. She was able to assure them that she had checked every corner, including the lavatories, and no one had been left anywhere in the store.

When she looked across again to where Andreas had been standing among some of the staff, he was not there. She went over to one of the women from the crystal and glassware department that he'd been standing next to.

'That man who was standing next to you? Did you see where he went?'

'You must be joking – in this crowd! But he asked about you.'

'Oh?'

'Yes, he asked what department you served in. I told him of course that you didn't serve in any department. You were a detective.'

Her heart sank.

'What did he say to that?'

The assistant laughed. 'One word – Police? And then he beat a hasty retreat. Was he one of your shoplifters?'

'I'll have to go,' Miss Eden said, 'and see if the police have found anything.'

She now was far more upset by Andreas finding out she was a detective than she was by the bomb scare. She knew it! She just knew that her job would put a man off. But surely he

100

might have met her and given her the chance to explain why she'd lied about it. Surely they could at least have been friends.

The police, helped by several sniffer dogs, had given the building a thorough search and found nothing, and so everyone was allowed to return. It was extremely difficult to get everyone settled back into their normal routine.

'It must have been a bloody hoax call!' Mr McKay sounded almost tearful. He was pale and shaking and she had to lead him upstairs to the canteen and fetch him a cup of tea. She began to wonder if she should have a word with Mrs Goodman herself. He definitely needed time off to get himself together again.

She sat down beside him at one of the canteen tables. A break for a cup of tea wouldn't do her any harm either, though it was not normal practice to sit in the canteen with the staff – even the manager. This, however, had not been a normal day.

'Who would want to do such a thing?' Mr McKay said.

'The police told me it was a woman's voice on the phone.'

'A dissatisfied customer, do you think? But surely not. We always do our best for customers. We very seldom have any complaints, and they are always dealt with very promptly and to the complete satisfaction of the customer.'

Miss Eden shrugged. 'Revenge of an ex-employee? Someone who was sacked?'

'That doesn't happen often either.'

After a few sips of tea, Mr McKay added, 'There was that girl who tried to steal the underwear. Her mother was angry at her dismissal, remember.'

Miss Eden looked unconvinced. 'Mmm. Maybe the mother, but I wouldn't think the girl . . .'

'The mother phoned.'

'Yes, I remember.'

'You should mention that to the police.'

'Yes, all right.'

She noticed how much Mr McKay's hand was trembling every time he lifted his cup. It occurred to her for the first time that he might have been drinking. It was remarkably common for people to drown their sorrows in drink. He could lose his job as a result of drinking. She decided, for his sake, she would keep a close eye on him from now on. If she found out that he was indeed over-indulging in alcohol, she would try her very best to help him.

After they finished their tea, he went to his office and she returned downstairs. Now she worried about Andreas. He knew where she lived, so hopefully he would contact her tonight, or sometime soon. If he thought anything of her at all, and he had seemed to like her very much, he surely would not just disappear.

Later, waiting alone in the flat in Springburn, her hopes faded. There was no contact the next day either. Or the next. At first, she couldn't understand it. All right, maybe a detective's job wasn't too attractive to a man. A bit off-putting, especially to someone a bit old-fashioned like Andreas, who liked ladies to be very feminine and probably dependent on their man. All the same, just to disappear like that wasn't fair, wasn't even polite, and he had such perfect manners. What with his bowing and hand-kissing and heel-clicking.

Gradually, grudgingly, she faced an alternative explanation. The man was either a con artist trying to get British citizenship, or a crook of some kind. After all, he didn't just echo the word 'detective' that the staff member from the crystal and glassware department had used. He said, 'Police!' then got off his mark.

What a fool she'd been. Later she relieved some of her anger and frustration in her karate class. She felt so glad the sensei said seniors could stay on after the class to work on focus pads. She partnered up with Brian, her usual sparring partner. She relaxed into fighting stance, weight evenly balanced, left hand leading, elbows tucked in. She exploded forward – left jab, right cross, thigh kick, right jab, left cross, thigh kick – moving smoothly forward, the sharp sock of skin on leather music to her ears. Sweat trickled down her face and her lungs pumped as she drove forward, letting her anger and aggression flow into the pads.

By Monday morning she felt much better. She was obviously well rid of the con artist. She'd had a narrow escape. She was concerned about Mr McKay, however. He looked worse. He looked as if he'd never slept and he had definitely been drinking. She had seen the results in enough people in her job to know the signs. While he was doing his usual routine of checking the departments, she slipped into his office. She noticed he'd begun to carry a large plastic carrier bag to work recently and suspected she'd find a bottle concealed in it. With that, she could confront him. That would be a first step in helping him. If she didn't do something to try and help him, any day now Mrs Goodman would notice and immediately dismiss him. She couldn't just stand aside and allow that to happen. Not to Mr McKay.

On opening the bag, she was astonished to find it packed with old clothes. There was also a bottle of Buckfast wine but it was the clothes that surprised and puzzled her. There was a stained, shabby pair of trousers, a grubby-looking shirt and coat, a khaki woollen balaclava and a pair of down-at-heel shoes. She couldn't understand it. She returned everything to the bag and quietly left the office.

She couldn't get the discovery out of her mind. Could it be that Mr McKay was leading a double life? Was he living like a tramp every night after leaving the shop? Was he changing into the old clothes and putting his day clothes into the carrier bag and carrying them around with him?

It seemed a crazy thing to do, but as his change of appearance and behaviour had only begun after the death of his wife, she thought it must be the result of his grief. She felt terribly sorry for him. She decided to watch him and follow him after he left the shop.

Before she got a chance to do this, incredibly, there was another bomb scare. It was absolutely terrible. She was sure thieves were having a field day lifting stuff on their way out, unseen among the mass of people being evacuated. Again she had to take charge of everything but this time she asked the police if they had recorded the telephone message, and they had. She then asked if she could go to the police station and listen to it. They agreed and, as she sat in the station listening to the recording, it came to her who the voice belonged to. Without a doubt it was the voice of the girl who had been dismissed for reeking of alcohol every day at work, and who had hidden her whisky in the lavatory cistern.

'I recognise her,' she told the policeman working the recorder. 'It's a girl who was sacked for drinking on the premises. We've still got her name and address on file.'

'We'll get that from you, and then pay her a visit.'

'That won't be enough to convict her, will it? Just my say-so?'

'Don't worry. Once we give her a visit and have a talk with her, you won't be bothered with her again.'

She was very relieved about that. A bomb scare every week would soon, one way or another, have led to the ruination of the business.

Now she just had Mr McKay to worry about. By the time she returned to the shop, however, it was locked up and Mr McKay had gone. But there would be other days. She was a very determined woman.

17

'Moira, I'm so sorry.' Sam Webster looked the picture of wretchedness.

'Why? What's wrong?'

'I'm genuinely ashamed.'

'What on earth have you done? Have you lost your job? Surely not. You're one of the best employees Goodmans have. Mrs Goodman said so herself.'

'No, it's worse than that. Oh, Moira, please forgive me.'

'For pity's sake, Sam, tell me what's happened.'

He hesitated, then blurted out, 'The B. & B. – The Floral. I didn't go there the last time because the woman in The Floral had come on to me. I mean, really come on to me. I told her I was happily married and loved my wife. I told her I was never going back to her B. & B. But . . . oh, what's the use of making excuses, Moira. That first time, I slept with her. I immediately regretted it. I told her that she meant nothing to me. I told her, but she's a determined woman. She keeps trying to contact me.'

There was a long silence. Eventually Moira said, 'I can't pretend I'm not hurt and disappointed, but I think I can understand – being away from home so much, I suppose you get lonely. I know I do.'

'Oh, Moira.' He rose and took a step towards her, arms

outstretched, eager to embrace her, but she stopped him in his tracks.

'No, Sam. You'll have to give me time. It's still been a shock. I can't just immediately carry on as if nothing has happened.'

'No, of course not, darling. But I promise you it'll never happen again. I regret it so much and I'm so very sorry.'

Moira looked miserable and tight-mouthed. But she nodded, then heaved herself out of her chair.

'I'll go and put the kettle on.'

After his wife had left the room, Sam cradled his head in his hands. He hated himself but at the same time he felt intense relief that he had managed to get it off his chest. At least now, Viv's threats to tell his wife didn't matter. If Viv contacted him and tried to threaten him again, he could now say, 'She knows.'

Even if Viv turned up at the store, he could still say, 'It doesn't matter what you say now. I don't care.'

He did care, that was the trouble. It was terrible to see Moira so unhappy. Every aspect of his life recently had become unexpectedly more difficult. Mrs Goodman seemed to have become cooler to him and more critical. Indeed, she seemed to be concentrating unusual and questioning attention on all the buyers these days. And of course the bomb scares had caused a complete upheaval, absolute chaos. The manager was pretty useless these days and the store detective wasn't in a good mood either. No doubt that was because of the extra goods that had gone missing during the bomb scares. He dreaded to think what would happen if there was yet another one.

He gazed around the comfortable sitting room, with its deep, cream-coloured leather chairs and settee, piled with colourful red and gold cushions. There were frosted glass doors leading into the dining room and the dining room had a hatch into the kitchen. They had had many a good party meal in the dining room. Betty and Alice enjoyed inviting friends along.

Moira knew all the neighbours and they took turns of having coffee together in each other's houses most mornings. Both he and Moira were members of the local bridge club and often enjoyed a game with some of the neighbours.

They all had a busy and happy life, especially a happy family life. He must have been mad to put it at risk. He'd had no feelings for Viv. Now he had. He hated her. But his hatred of her was not nearly as strong as his hatred of himself.

Moira returned to the room carrying a tray. Immediately he got up and lifted the tray from her, and set it down on the coffee table.

'I'll see to it,' Moira said, and began arranging the cups and saucers and pouring out the tea.

'And how was your day?' she queried, after taking a few sips of her tea. She usually asked this, but never in such a cool, polite voice. He had always shared all his experiences with her. Except the one with Viv, until now.

'There was another bomb scare.'

Moira tutted. 'A hoax, do you think? They didn't find anything, did they?'

'No. Whoever it was must be mad to do a thing like that.'

Just then Betty and Alice came in. Betty said, 'We got everything you wanted, Mum. Plus some lovely wee profiteroles and cream sponges. Miniature ones. If we got too many, they'll keep in the freezer.'

It was then he remembered that some neighbours were coming in later with their families, who were friends of Betty and Alice. Alice was home for the weekend.

'Sounds delicious,' he said. 'When's everybody coming?'

'About eight or just after.'

After having a cup of tea, Moira and the girls went through to the kitchen to prepare the evening meal. He offered to help but was told just to keep out of the way.

'Go and watch TV or something.'

Then later, when Mr and Mrs Brown and Mr and Mrs Campbell and their daughters were in and settled in the sitting room, Mrs Campbell said, 'You'll have seen the evening paper?'

'No,' Moira said. 'The girls did the shopping and I forgot to tell them to get a paper. Why?'

'Oh, big pictures of all the crowds in Glassford Street and Wilson Street – even up to Ingram Street and down to Argyle Street. What a carry on. Were you there, Sam?'

'Yes. They didn't find anything though. Some mad hoaxer. I hope to God they catch him. It was a terrible upheaval.'

'Mrs Goodman must be very worried.'

'We all are.'

'I see her son is in the papers as well.'

'Oh? What's he been saying this time?'

'Oh, it was apparently in answer to letters about the cost of the building of the Scottish Parliament.'

'Well,' Moira said, 'it did cost a ridiculous amount of money.'

'I know,' Mrs Campbell agreed. 'But he was saying that the Dome in England had cost very much more and even a set of new offices down there had cost almost as much, and no one had been up in arms and complaining about the costs down south.'

'He's a great guy,' Sam said. 'He's never afraid of speaking his mind.'

The girls had gone upstairs to the attic room and the rhythmic beat of pop music could be heard echoing down the stairs.

'Anyone for a drink?' Sam asked. He needed a drink himself. With one thing and another, it had been a stressful day. He brought out a bottle of whisky, which he knew was a favourite with the men, and a bottle of vodka and some soft drinks as mixers for the ladies.

The evening went well but it was late before their friends left, and then Moira and the girls tidied up and filled the dishwasher. Later he and Moira lay in their separate beds in silence after saying goodnight. Moira's voice had been cool and polite again.

She had appeared and sounded perfectly normal earlier in the evening, though at one point Mrs Brown had said, 'Are you all right, Moira?'

'Yes. Why?'

'You look a bit strained around the eyes. I thought maybe you'd a headache. I've got some paracetamol in my bag if you need any.'

'No, no. But thanks all the same.'

He couldn't sleep and he suspected that she was lying awake in the dark as well.

The next day was Saturday, always a busy day, and he was glad that he had a lot to do – phone calls, correspondence to catch up with, and people to see. It was nearly closing time and Betty, thank goodness, had gone off to keep a date with a boyfriend, when Viv turned up. She'd asked downstairs for him, saying that a friend had arrived from down south to see him.

He braced himself for a confrontation but was determined it would not be in the store. He went downstairs and led her out, just as Mr McKay was about to lock the doors.

'Where are we going, darling? Are you taking me for a nice dinner?'

She was all cosy and clingy.

'No,' he said coldly. 'I'm taking you to the station and putting you on a train back to South Castle-on-Sea.'

Her coyness disappeared.

'You bastard. Don't you for one minute imagine that you're going to get away with this.'

'Look, Viv, how often do I have to tell you? We had sex. A

fling, I believe it's called, and it meant nothing. I'm a happily married man. You're just wasting your time.'

'You won't be so happily married once I have a chat with your wife.'

'My wife knows about you. I've told her. It's one of the risks of the job and being away from home so much. She's always known it. She's a strong woman and perfectly able to cope with the likes of you. So just fuck off!'

18

Show me the way to go home,
I'm tired and I want to go to bed,
I had a little drink about an hour ago,
And it's gone right to my head.
No matter where I roam,
On land or sea or foam,
You can always hear me singing this song,
Show me the way to go home.

The children clapped their hands. 'Sing another one, Granny.'

She was aware that half their enjoyment came from the fact that bedtime was being put off. 'All right. Just one more.'

Ali bali, ali bali bee,
Sitting on my mammy's knee,
Greetin' for a wee baw bee,
Tae buy some coulter's candy.

'Just one more, Granny.'

She laughed. 'Well, this is the very last one for tonight. It's way past your bedtime now.'

At the back of the Central Hotel,
There a man with a nose like a bell.
If you want it to ting,
You pull a wee string,
At the back of the Central Hotel.

The children giggled and then shouted, 'Another last one, Granny.'

'Well, just a wee story this time.'

Then, after telling them one of her made-up stories, she said firmly, 'Come on now. I'll be getting a row from Nanny if I keep you up any longer. I'll come back again soon, I promise.'

She kissed them goodnight and tucked them into bed, before going to tell the nanny that she was leaving.

George Square was busy with people getting home from work, either in cars or buses or walking up to Queen Street Station. Towering over the Square on the east side was the magnificent City Chambers. In front was the Cenotaph, which always made her sad when she looked at it. It represented so much grief. It stood for so many young people whose lives had been cut off, wasted. And young lives were still being sacrificed. Would the powers that be never learn? John said it was all based on lies. It was about oil and greed more than anything. Blair and Bush were liars. One thing was for sure – she wasn't going to vote Labour after the recent debacle in Iraq. People argued that the Labour government had done a lot of good, especially for old people, and so they had, but the war, and Blair's shoulder-to-shoulder attitude with Bush, had sickened a lot of people and turned them off.

She felt tired but reluctant to face the empty house in Huntershill. She was tempted just to sit on one of the benches in the Square and watch the world go by. But there was no use postponing the evil hour. Her loneliness and gathering cloud of depression had to be faced. She struggled to be positive and brave as she made her way up to the station. There was a taxi rank at each end of the station, and usually plenty of taxis available.

As it turned out, there was a queue at the first rank. She walked through the noisy, echoing station to where the other rank was situated, and caught a cab there. As it whizzed along the dual carriageway, she felt like telling the driver to slow down. She was in no hurry to get home. In no time, however, he was swinging up the thick, bush- and tree-lined drive of the house. It occurred to her that she should get a gardener in to tame the place. Everything had got wild and out of hand. Bushes and plants were crowding against the walls, and branches of trees were tapping against the upstairs windows.

She forced herself once more to consider selling the place and buying a flat in town. She could even try for a flat in George Square and be near to the children all the time. She feared that she would not be able to cling so closely to the visible memories of Tom for much longer. Not here, at least. In the store, it was different. She would continue to fight to keep Goodmans of Glassford Street as Tom Goodman had always kept it, and to run it as he had always wanted it to be run.

Once in the sitting room, she switched on the lights and stood gazing up at the portrait of Tom Goodman Senior. There was quite a strong resemblance to her Tom in the features, but Tom Senior was of a heavier build. She had always liked tall, lean men and her Tom had been tall and lean. That was why Horatio in *CSI: Miami* always reminded her of Tom. But there was also the tenderness, the caring, and the passionate sex they had always shared.

She went over and tugged at the curtains, in an effort to protect herself from the black wilderness outside. Then she switched on the television to give at least the illusion of company.

Nevertheless, depression increased and in a desperate effort to reawaken the happy time with the children, she began singing, defiantly, over the noise of the television:

Who saw the 42nd, who saw them sailing away?
Who saw the 42nd, sailing down the Broomielaw?
Some of them had kilts in tatters,
Some of them had none at all.
Some of them had dirks and stockings,
Sailing down the Broomielaw.

She began rocking herself backwards and forwards.

Ah'm a skyscraper wean, ah live on the nineteenth flair.
But ah'm no gawn oot tae play any mair,
Cause since we've moved tae Castlemilk, ah'm wastin' away
Cause ah'm getting' wan meal less every day.

Oh ye cannae fling pieces oot a twenty storey flat,
Seven hundred hungry weans'll testify tae that.
If it's butter, cheese or jeely, if the bread is plain or pan,
The odds against it reachin' earth are ninety-nine tae wan . . .

Tears spilled over and she repeated the words like a mantra as she rocked herself and clutched her hands together.

Ah'm a skyscraper wean . . .
Ah'm a skyscraper wean . . .

'The Jeely Piece Song' reminded her of her own tenement upbringing. It made her sadder than ever to be reminded of the close and loving relationship she'd once had with her mother and father, and the friendship and neighbourliness of the other tenants in the building. Her mother and father had been so proud of her, first getting a job in Goodmans, then getting promoted to window dressing, and then – joy of joys – marrying such a lovely man, and *the boss*, to cap it all. Tom had been good to her mother, especially after her father died, and even wanted to buy her a bungalow or a cottage somewhere. But her mother had refused to leave her wee tenement flat.

'No thanks, son,' she'd said. 'It's a kind thought, and I appreciate it, but all my happy memories of my husband are here and I've so many good friends in the building.'

Her mother had clung to the memories of her husband just as she was now clinging to the memories of Tom. Her mother had been surrounded by friends and neighbours, though, to keep her happy. And she had a good son-in-law. It was a different situation with herself. Douglas Benson was an ambitious, ruthless man, who hated her. She was so tied up in the business and in trying to protect it, that she had no life or friends outside it. And this house was so lonely and isolated, she had not even any neighbours to turn to. It was getting harder to believe that she had once been happy here.

She wondered what Benson would think of her selling the house and buying a flat in George Square, or in one of the streets nearby. It would mean, of course, that she would be nearer to Glassford Street and the store. He would not like that aspect of a move.

She kept rocking herself backwards and forwards, not knowing what to do. If Minna had been stronger and closer to her, life would have been more bearable. But it seemed she'd lost a daughter as well as a husband. Often, she worried about Minna. Minna professed love for Douglas and was one hundred per cent loyal to him, but could it be that Minna was also afraid of him, and if so – why? He was a bully, of course, and no doubt he always had to have his own way. She didn't allow him to succeed in bullying her, but Minna had never been able to stand up to him.

Poor Minna. She wept for her as well as for herself.

Eventually, exhausted, she dried her tears and went into the kitchen to make herself a soothing milky drink. She was ashamed of feeling sorry for herself and determined to make a concentrated effort to pull herself together. After a good night's sleep, she'd be more able to decide what to do for the best.

She didn't get a good night's sleep, of course, and lay listening to the trees tapping and scraping at the window for what felt like hours.

The next day, after the staff meeting, she decided to go to the nearest estate agent's office and see what the housing situation was in the area. It might be difficult or even impossible to buy a flat in or near George Square. It was a very sought-after area.

She'd go to Edinburgh as soon as possible and find out what John thought about the idea of her moving house. Before she had the opportunity to do so, however, she had a very upsetting phone call from John.

'Mum, you'll never guess what's happened.'

'You sound upset, son. What's wrong?'

'I didn't phone you earlier because I didn't want to upset you, but Julie, my secretary, has been murdered.'

'Murdered?' Abi echoed loudly in disbelief.

'She was found by a neighbour who had a key. I had gone to the flat, but she didn't answer the door. She must have been lying inside, already dead.'

'Johnny, how awful! No wonder you're upset.'

'The police have been questioning me.'

'What do you mean? They surely don't think you had anything to do with it? They couldn't.'

'I can't believe it either, and I suppose they've been questioning other people – neighbours, friends, and people like that. But I didn't like their attitude towards me. They seemed very suspicious, to say the least.'

'But that's ridiculous.'

'I know.'

'The only reason I can think of is that we were together a lot – in the Parliament and out of it. She travelled with me to my constituency and various engagements.'

'That was her job.'

'I know. But they keep coming to question me at the flat. It's only a couple of closes from Julie's. Now they've asked me to come to the station – "to help with their enquiries", they say. But I'm worried, Mum.'

Now all her worries about moving house and everything else were banished from her mind. All she cared about was her son.

19

Mr McKay changed into his tramp's clothes in the nearest public toilet. Then, with the balaclava partly covering his face, he returned to the street and shuffled along, his carrier bag slung over one arm. He was grateful he didn't need to go home and sit for a whole evening by himself, at the mercy of agonising grief and guilt. Near here, he remembered seeing homeless men in a cul-de-sac off Argyle Street. There had been a ledge jutting out from the back of one of the buildings meant to shelter the refuse bins. The men had moved the bins and were squatting under the ledge on layers of cardboard. The bitter wind cut savagely through the thin material of Mr McKay's second-hand jacket. He hunched his shoulders, his head settling deeply into the flimsy collar.

The smell of stale wine and decaying vegetables told him he was nearly there. Turning the corner of the derelict warehouse, he saw the glow of the fire bravely defying the cold and damp. Huge shadows lurched menacingly across the shabby brick walls, out of all proportion to the small and insignificant figures that huddled in protective sympathy around the burning timbers.

He called out a hoarse greeting to warn them of his arrival. They were all too easily scared these days, succumbing to the predatory attacks of thrill-seeking 'neds'. The cold had already numbed his lips, making conversation difficult.

To grunts of appreciation, he struggled to release the bottle of Buckfast from the confines of his jacket, frozen fingers slipping hesitantly over the screw top, soon to release oblivion and acceptance.

Mr McKay took a swig of his wine and the men visibly brightened. One said, 'Gie's a swig o' yer Buckie, pal.'

Mr McKay handed him the bottle. 'Pass it round.'

The three men drank deeply from it before returning it to him. As he joined them on the cardboard, he surreptitiously wiped the bottle before putting it to his mouth again.

'Have we seen you here before?' the eldest of the group mumbled. His hair was long and dirty white and he looked as if he was wearing two or three coats, the top one tied round the waist with string.

'Been out Springburn way. Walked in tonight.'

'You must be knackered.'

He nodded, then took another drink before handing the bottle round again. They drank from it gratefully and he could see he was accepted as their friend as a result.

'Where are you from yourselves?'

One of them said, 'Edinburgh. But I couldnae get a minute's peace there for the polis. Always movin' ye on.'

'Aye,' the old man said. 'At least ye get a bit o' peace here, and there's always the Salvation Army.'

'Or the Quakers,' the other man added.

'What do they do? I've never come across them.'

'Oh, ye will have, but they dinnae wear a uniform or anythin', and they dinnae try tae convert ye, or save ye, or any carry on like that. They dish out soup an' sandwiches most nights in the Square. I didnae know who they were either till I asked around.'

'The Sally Army's OK.' The old man's voice turned nasty. 'They sometimes can get you a bed.'

'I never said anything against the Sally Army.'

'Here,' Mr McKay interrupted. 'Have another drink.'

'What's your handle?' One of them wiped his mouth. 'Eh?'

'Your name – Dopey, is it?'

'Oh. Mac. Mac'll do fine.'

'Well, yer Buckie's smashin', Mac. Warms the cockles of yer heart, so it does. You can come here any night, pal.'

After the bottle had done a few more rounds and was empty, their voices became slurred. They spoke about everything from football to their fond memories of relaxing in the comfortable warmth of libraries. The huge, domed Mitchell Library in Glasgow, the biggest reference library in Europe, had been their favourite.

'Used to be great in there but now it's all been gutted and changed. You don't know where you are in it now or where to go. I went into it one day and there was nothing but paintings on the ground floor. Not a book or a comfy armchair in sight. I don't know what they're playing at. Not a book in sight, and before I could go upstairs and look there, a bloody security guard came and chucked me out.'

'Undemocratic,' Mr McKay managed. Although he secretly thought the guard had been quite right. Who in their right mind would want a filthy, flea-ridden tramp wandering about the place? He remembered that exhibition. Jenny had not really been well enough to go but she had insisted that he take her. If he remembered correctly, it was an exhibition of Avril Paton's paintings. She was the one who had originally become famous for her paintings of Glasgow tenements. He liked those, but she had now branched out into modern stuff – none of which he either understood or appreciated. Jenny did, though. She loved them all and enjoyed the event. Afterwards, of course, she had been so exhausted and unwell, he had to send for the doctor. But despite this, she said it had been worth it.

He struggled to his feet. He hadn't had enough wine to completely blot out his thoughts.

'I'm away to try and get another bottle.'

'Good man, Mac,' was the general consensus.

He stumbled away.

It was strange how different Glasgow seemed after dark, especially late at night. There was an unexpected number of people walking around. Groups of young people laughing and talking. He'd heard that young people only went out after ten in the evening and gathered in discos and nightclubs to dance and drink away the night. Apparently, the busiest time for taxi drivers was three in the morning when the clubs all spilled out. One taxi driver had said that the drunk girls were worse than the boys. And once they were in the cab, he couldn't get them out. Even in one case when a girl was sick in the cab but refused to be put out.

'I'll sue if you touch me,' she'd threatened. 'I'll cry rape.'

Though Mr McKay doubted the police would believe a girl like that. The police, he believed, would be more likely to take the taxi driver's word. There were lots of perfectly respectable and nice girls on the staff at Goodmans and he liked to cling to the view that girls should not all be tarred with the same brush.

There had been Goodmans Christmas dinners held in different places over the years for the staff. Mrs Goodman always picked the venue and he was always amazed at the number of excellent and interesting eating places there were in Glasgow, especially in the Merchant City area. Last year had been a real surprise for him. Mrs Goodman had booked them in at Arta – where the old cheese market had been. It had such an unimposing exterior and entry by a small wooden door. But once opened, it revealed a vast space where white Italian statues stood and a face on one wall spouted water. Upstairs, long tables had been set out for them. Give Mrs Goodman her due, he thought, she could be a bit eccentric and ruthless at times; nevertheless she was good to her staff. The thought never failed to plague him with terrible guilt. He should have gone down on his knees to the bank manager and pleaded for the necessary money, thought of some way rather than stealing from Mrs Goodman. But he hadn't been thinking straight. He had been demented with worry and time had been fast running out. Even faster than he'd expected, in the end. He suffered guilt about that too. Moving Jenny from her own bed and having her travel across the city to a strange place had been too much for her. He had no doubts about that now.

He had done all the wrong things.

He couldn't get the other bottle of wine quickly enough. He opened the bottle immediately and drank deeply, gratefully, from it. Then, somehow, he found his way back to where the other men were hopefully waiting.

'Oh, here, ye're a right pal, so ye are,' they greeted him as he held out the bottle to be passed around. Later the men all dozed off under protective sheets of cardboard. He dozed too but he knew that somehow he had to get home so that he could have a bath and shave and try to make himself look respectable for starting work in the shop.

He had a terrible problem getting a taxi. He tried hailing several but no one would stop for him. Eventually he had to go to a rank and offer the driver the fare, plus a tip, before he would agree to let him into the cab. In Bishopbriggs, he practically fell out of the vehicle and was glad that the villa was comparatively isolated, with no next-door neighbours to see him. It was a terrible problem getting the key in the lock but eventually he managed it and stumbled into the house. How he hated it now! He made it to the bedroom and flopped onto the bed.

Mercifully, that was the last he remembered until morning. Then, despite his thumping headache and parched mouth, he bathed and dressed in his proper clothes, phoned for a taxi and arrived at the store late but thankfully before Mrs Goodman or the Bensons. The cleaners were standing outside, however, and not looking too pleased.

'I'm sorry, ladies,' he said as he unlocked the gates and pushed them back. 'I slept in.' Hastily he opened the other doors and switched on all the lights. Then he went up in the lift to his office and left his plastic carrier bag containing his shabby clothes on his desk. He was breathless and his heart was palpitating with rushing to get everything done, as he returned downstairs to check the rest of the staff arriving. Only Miss Eden seemed to notice his distress.

'Are you all right, Mr McKay?'

He fiddled with his glasses and avoided her eyes.

'Yes, fine, fine.'

'You don't look well at all.'

'It's just a headache, Miss Eden. And I've taken a couple of tablets. They'll soon do the trick.'

She didn't look satisfied and it was with obvious reluctance that she walked away and went upstairs to her office. Soon he realised he really needed to take something for his headache and he sent one of the juniors out for some painkillers. They helped a little and, after a cup of tea, he was able to go round and check every department. Then back upstairs, he made some phone calls before attending Mrs Goodman's usual staff meeting. He shrank into a seat at the back, behind other senior staff members. He usually sat in the front row but he was afraid that Mrs Goodman, like Miss Eden, would notice his condition and question him about it.

However, Mrs Goodman seemed to have other things on

her mind and the meeting was an unusually short one. She was quite abrupt, in fact, and there were murmurings as they left of 'What was wrong with her?'

Later he was downstairs discussing stock in Jewellery when he saw Mrs Goodman hurrying away outside to a waiting taxi. She seemed quite agitated and he wondered then like the others what on earth could be wrong. It didn't seem likely that it was anything to do with the store. Everything was fine as far as he was aware, except that Douglas Benson had been talking about modernisation, but that was his usual thing. He wondered if it was something to do with another member of her family – John Goodman, for example. He was always in some sort of hot water with his extreme views.

However, Mr McKay had enough to worry about, coping with his own situation. He must remember to buy another bottle of wine for tonight.

20

Miss Eden watched the three children who had walked in along with a respectable-looking couple. This was a trick of young shoplifters – to come in alongside adults in an effort to look as if they were family and avoid the suspicion that they would cause by appearing in the store on their own. She had caught children doing this more than once.

Today, as she watched them, she was wearing a blonde wig and a tan-coloured duffel coat. She kept quite a wardrobe of disguises upstairs in her office – not only clothes and shoes, but handbags, hats, scarves and wigs. There were also different kinds of cosmetics. As she had suspected, after a few minutes, the children separated from the adults and began sidling around the counters, peering at the goods and giving quick glances to see if anyone was watching them.

The trouble with young thieves was that they were fast runners. The moment they reached the doors, they were off like hares on a dog track. She used her mobile to alert the security guard at the door and surreptitiously followed the children. The ground floor was usually their favourite. For one thing, it was easier to make a quick escape from there. Also, most of the goods on the ground floor departments were smaller and easier to grab and carry or secrete in clothing – like jewellery, perfume, gloves, and so on.

This time they tried a new ploy. Two of them started a noisy fight, which distracted the assistants and the nearby customers, while the third child helped himself to the contents of a box of jewellery. Miss Eden immediately ran towards the boy but he saw her coming and was off like a shot. She flew after him, bashing open the doors and racing down Glassford Street to Argyle Street. Unfortunately, Argyle Street was packed with shoppers and it was easier for a child to nip in and out of the mob of people than it was for her. Soon she had lost him.

It was really infuriating, a bad start to the day. The favourite times for thieves of all ages were early morning and late at night. Early in the morning, the shop was comparatively quiet, and assistants all tended to be talking about what they'd done the night before. At the end of the day, they were tired, they were tidying up and maybe talking about what they were going to do that night.

Returning to the shop – still slightly breathless – she saw a woman enter carrying a large Debenhams shopping bag. This could mean she'd just come across from Debenhams where she'd made a perfectly normal purchase, and that was what the bag contained. On the other hand, it could be an empty bag lined with tin foil. If the bag was lined with foil, the alarm would not go off if she tried to take stolen merchandise out of the shop. The foil did something to the tag on the goods. Miss Eden watched the woman and, sure enough, upstairs in the fashion department, she saw her slip a couple of designer label dresses into the bag, then saunter away back to the lift. She joined the woman and stood at the back of the lift filled with customers and returned to the ground floor. Then she followed the woman while once again taking out her mobile to alert the security guard.

This time, with the help of the security guard, she caught the woman. Then it was up to the manager's office. Mr McKay

126

looked as if he had been asleep at his desk and had awakened with a start when she rapped on his door.

The police were sent for. Then there were the usual reports to be written up. Downstairs again, she got her eye on a man who answered the description that Frasers had passed about. There was always good cooperation between the detectives in other stores, and this call had described a man who had stolen from them in the past. He hadn't got away with anything today, but no doubt he'd try another store. So she began following him around. Eventually he must have realised this because he faced her and said, 'God, are you the store tec? A nice looking bird like you?'

Not long after that, she saw a young woman lift some cosmetics, followed her outside and stopped her. The woman immediately threatened, 'I'm going to stab you with this needle.'

A quick karate chop removed the needle, but Miss Eden had to listen to a stream of filthy and abusive language, all the way to the manager's office, and until the police came and hauled the woman away.

Care had constantly to be taken by the staff nowadays, with the drug problem being so bad. Often, the girls would be stacking shelves or tidying jumpers or other goods at night, and they would find needles. Some girls had become so nervous about this that they had left as a result.

Miss Eden went along to The Granary for a late lunch of a bowl of soup and a sandwich. As she sat absently stirring the soup and waiting for it to cool, her thoughts strayed first to Andreas. She wondered what he was up to. Probably she'd had a lucky escape. Then her thoughts turned to Mr McKay and she wondered what was happening to him. The poor man was disintegrating before her eyes. She suspected that if Mrs Goodman had not been taking an unusual amount of time off recently and seemed to have things other than business on her mind, he would have been sacked.

She wondered what she could do to help him. She couldn't bring his wife back, but surely there must be some way to give him the help and support he obviously needed. First she had to find out exactly what he was doing. And stop him doing it. Even if she had to stop him against his will. Drink had fuddled his brain and affected his health. The poor man didn't know what he was doing. This was one of her early shifts and she had been busy all morning. No doubt she'd be kept busy for another couple of hours, and already she was tired.

Nevertheless, there was no time to waste as far as Mr McKay was concerned. She'd have to start right away – tonight. She wouldn't go home. She'd have a walk about the town and go somewhere for a cup of tea, then she'd come back when it was store closing time and try to catch Mr McKay coming out, so that she could follow him. If she could follow him and find out exactly what he was doing, she would have a better idea of how she could help him.

After her lunch, she did her couple of hours and reported off duty to Mr McKay. He looked so miserable and pathetic, giving her a half-smile and barely managing his usual 'Thank you, Miss Eden. Have a nice evening.'

She felt her determination strengthen. She was strong enough for both of them. She would get him back to normal if it was the last thing she did.

Once outside, she first of all took a walk along to Argyle Street, looking in Marks & Spencer's window. She also looked at the plaque that commemorated the fact that Marks & Spencer's stood on the site of the Black Bull Inn, where Robert Burns had once stayed and where he wrote to Agnes McLehose.

'I've never had any romance in my life,' Miss Eden thought, 'and no doubt I never will.' The thought didn't depress her.

She had a good life. She turned away from the plaque and began walking along towards the High Street, one of the oldest streets in the city. There were plenty of stories of romance connected with it. And other things too, of course.

Walking up the High Street towards Castle Street, she passed the site of the old university. The old university had been involved in sensational anatomical experiments. In 1818 Professor Jeffrey publicly showed the journey of electricity through the body using what he called the Galvanic Battery he'd invented. He sat a corpse in a chair and when the Galvanic Battery was switched on, the audience was horrified to see the body appear as if it had come to life. Apparently, the novelist Mary Shelley had been in the audience and it was said that it was this incident that inspired her to write her Gothic horror novel, *Frankenstein.*

Many famous writers originated in Glasgow, and in this area there was a plaque commemorating the poet Thomas Campbell, whose friends were among the greatest writers of the age, like Sir Walter Scott, Wordsworth, Coleridge, Byron and Keats. There was a statue of Campbell in George Square and he was buried in Poets' Corner in Westminster Abbey.

Miss Eden did not read much poetry but she often found pleasure in books, especially novels. She usually read at night until she felt too sleepy and had to switch off her bedside lamp. Thinking of books reminded her of the first free library in Scotland. That was thanks to Walter Stirling, a Glasgow merchant who, in 1791, left to the city his house in Milton Street, a share of the Tontine South, his collection of eight hundred and four books and one thousand pounds for the purpose of maintaining 'the constant and perpetual existence of a Public Library for the citizens or inhabitants of Glasgow'. After that, other generous folk of Glasgow donated books until the collection had grown, by 1891, from eight hundred and four to upwards of forty-six thousand.

Miss Eden now looked over at the St Mungo Museum of Religious Life and Art. She'd been there quite a few times and found it interesting. It was a great place for schools and other groups, of course, to find out about religion and art across the world and to promote respect between people of different faiths and of none.

Next to it was the Cathedral with its pre-Reformation Gothic architecture. It had survived intact from the ravages of the 1560 Reformation because it was defended by local Glaswegians who were fiercely proud of it. Moreover, St Kentigern, Glasgow's patron saint, was buried there.

She supposed she came into the category of no religion. She had never gone to any church since she was a child and regularly attended Sunday School in her best clothes and shoes. Everybody did in those days. Nowadays, she had become too sceptical – caused, no doubt, by having to deal with so many crooks, liars, thieves and con artists. It was enough to make anyone lose faith – in human nature, anyway.

Across from the Cathedral was Provand's Lordship, the only medieval house still standing in the city. This was where Mary, Queen of Scots stayed when visiting her husband, Lord Darnley, who was ill with the pox. She remembered reading about Mary. What a sad life she'd had.

Miss Eden suddenly felt exhausted. It had been a hard day. She turned to go back down the High Street and find some place decent to have a cup of tea and a sandwich before making for Goodmans. Or perhaps she would wait across the road in the multi-storey car park. She kept checking her watch as she drank a cup of tea and munched at a salad sandwich. She had to time it right. She had to be positioned near the store to watch for Mr McKay coming out.

She ended up against a wall in the shadows of the entrance to the car park, and eventually saw Mr McKay emerge dressed in his business suit, striped shirt, collar and tie. He was carrying a plastic shopping bag. He walked down to Argyle Street and she slipped from the shadows and followed him. He went to the nearest public lavatory and after a time emerged transformed into a shabby tramp. She wouldn't have known him except for his glasses and the fact that she'd seen the shabby clothes in his carrier bag in the office. He took on a slow shuffling gait as he progressed along Argyle Street until he turned into an area of back entrances of surrounding shops. On drawing nearer, Miss Eden heard cries of, 'Oh, it's you, Mac. Come on in. Have you got the Buckie? Good man!'

She waited for a while before looking in. There was a little group of what would no doubt be homeless men. They were passing round a bottle and each of them, including Mr McKay, was taking his gulps of wine from it. Miss Eden walked quietly away.

As far as she was concerned, this was the last night Mr McKay would behave like this.

She would see to it.

21

As Abi was waiting for John, the tour guide was saying to a crowd of people, 'Before we go on the tour, please come forward and look at the modern sculpture. It's called "The Honours of Scotland" and the Queen gave it to Parliament when she opened the building. Some of you may have seen this on television – it was commissioned by the Corporation of Gold and Silversmiths of Edinburgh and was called "The Honours".' He looked around enquiringly. 'What are these? The Crown Jewels of Scotland . . . you have to use your imagination. That's the crown, the sword through the middle, and the gilded bit is the sceptre. So "The Honours of Scotland", perhaps reminding us that when Scotland's Parliament sat before the union with England, the crown was sometimes taken into Parliament Hall, the Parliament buildings, as a symbol of royal authority.'

Abi tried to peer through the crowd for a glimpse of John, but without success. She began to wonder if she was waiting in the wrong place, especially when she heard the tour guide saying, 'For those who work in the building, there's a coffee bar and restaurant. A lot of people work in the building. It's not just MSPs. They have researchers and assistants. There's security, catering, cleaning, computer services . . .'

Was it the restaurant John had said to go to and wait for

him? She was so upset and worried after he phoned, she couldn't remember for sure. It was when she was walking towards the restaurant that she saw John. His tall figure came striding towards her.

'Sorry to keep you waiting, Mum. It's been one hell of a day in the chamber and what with this other horrible business . . .' He took her arm. 'Come on, we'll go and have a cup of tea.'

Once they were settled with their tea at a table, she asked, 'What on earth has been happening? Why should the police be pestering you?'

'Oh, they've been questioning others as well, but you see, I've been closest to her. I mean, with her always being with me – in the office and travelling around. I even live near her. I suppose I can understand their attitude. But all the same . . .'

'I know. The tour guide was just saying there's lots of people work in the building. It's not just MSPs.'

'I've even been in her house. I had dinner with her there not so long ago. But there was nothing going on between us. Nothing personal. She was a nice girl but I just wasn't interested in anything personal. To be honest, I didn't fancy her. Anyway, we've been hell of a busy working towards the next election. She was so sure, so optimistic, that the Nationalists were going to wipe the board with Labour next time, and so was I.' He rubbed his fingers through his hair. 'Who on earth could have done this, Mum?'

'Had she a boyfriend?'

'As I say, neither of us had much time for a personal life. But now that you mention it, there had been somebody at one time. Oh, it was a good while back, though. She'd packed him in. But I did wonder at the time what on earth she saw in him. He was nothing much to look at – as bald as a coot. Of course that's the fashion these days. I've never heard her speak of him for ages. I'd forgotten about him. I'm sure she'd never seen or heard from him. She certainly never mentioned him to me. I don't think that can have anything to do with her murder. As I say, what happened with him was a long time ago.'

'Did you tell the police?'

'No.'

'John, he might be one of these obsessive people who never give up a relationship, who just refuse to believe it when someone rejects them.'

'I doubt it, Mum. After all this time?'

'Son, will you please do as I say? Have a word with the police.' She forced her voice to sound positive, even cheerful. 'I'm sure that'll help in their enquiries, dear. Now drink up your tea and tell me what's been happening in the chamber.'

He hesitated. 'Oh well, OK. I'll speak to the police.'

'Good. Now stop worrying and tell me what's been going on in the chamber.'

He sighed. 'Another argument about Trident. I'm against having it, as you know. And remember how the former diplomat, Hans Blix, warned Blair and Bush against thinking Saddam Hussein had weapons of mass destruction. Of course, they ignored him. They knew better. And the rest is history.' He groaned and shook his head. 'When I think of all the young men killed as a result. Not to mention all the innocent civilians.'

'I know, son, it's wicked.'

'Blix was right about Iraq and I bet he'll be proved right about Trident. He says some experts reckon it'll cost us seventy-six billion pounds over thirty years. And how is that supposed to honour the non-proliferation treaty?'

He then listed all the countries that now had nuclear weapons and ended with, 'No wonder the non-nuclear countries are showing enormous resentment.'

'Yes,' his mother agreed. 'I remember seeing pictures of Nagasaki and Hiroshima.' She shuddered. 'Absolutely dreadful.'

'Now you're getting upset. I'm sorry, Mum, and I haven't even offered you anything to eat. Let me get you a sandwich. Or something more substantial? There's nice macaroni cheese. I know you like that.'

'No, son. Thanks all the same. I don't feel hungry.'

'I shouldn't be worrying you like this. What with my work and now my personal problems as well . . .'

'Don't be daft. Who better to talk to and confide in than your mother? No, no, dear. I want you always to feel free to talk to me. I'd be very hurt and upset if you didn't.'

'Thanks, Mum. I feel better already about the police questioning me. Maybe you're right. About Julie's ex-boyfriend, I mean. There's no telling the extremes that some people will go to. It seems a bit far-fetched to me but as I say, you never know. I'll certainly contact the police right away.'

'Good. Now you can pour me out another cup of tea.'

He grinned at her. 'You're a right tea jenny. By the way, have you done anything yet about my suggestion?'

'What suggestion?'

'About getting a book made of all your songs and poems and stories.'

'Those daft things? Who'd be interested in them?'

'I was, and so are your grandchildren, and so were innumerable Scottish children of previous generations. It would be a pity to let them die out. To have them recorded in a book would keep them alive for future generations.'

'But who would want to publish such daft things, son? And as far as the wee stories are concerned, I just make them up.'

'That's great. Scottish publishers would be interested. There's quite a few of them you could try. You've got a computer in the office, haven't you?'

'Yes, of course.'

'Well, get your stories and songs on to the computer, either in the office or at home. Especially at home. It would give you something worthwhile to do in the evenings, instead of always watching television.'

'I'll think about it, son.'

'*Do* it, Mum.'

She laughed. 'Oh, all right then.' Though she wasn't keen on computers and preferred to write in longhand.

'Good.'

She enjoyed her visit, as she always did when she went to see John, despite the worrying side of their conversation on this occasion. However, now that she knew about Julie's ex-boyfriend, she felt better, more confident. The police would be interested in him, she felt sure. They would do all they could to find him and bring him in to – as they say – 'help with their enquiries'.

There had been several awful cases in the past reported in the papers where ex-boyfriends or ex-partners had tormented and even murdered the person who had rejected them. She had to smile, remembering John's idea of making a book of all the nonsense she entertained the children with. She didn't believe for a minute that any publisher would want to publish them. However, she'd promised John she would put them all together, so she'd try, just to please him.

She decided it was hardly worthwhile going back to the store. She would go to visit the children instead, and stay in the penthouse for a few hours. However, when she pressed the penthouse buzzer, there was no reply. She felt suddenly desolate. Of course, it was the run-up to Christmas and there was a lot going on in the city, including parties and pantomimes. No doubt they were enjoying themselves somewhere and didn't need any entertainment from her.

The Square was beautifully lit up with lights in the shape of bells shining from high poles all along each side, and they swung back and forth as if they were ringing. The buildings were floodlit. There was a beautiful nativity scene in a glass house with a silver roof. Rather incongruously, there were shows nearby belting out raucous music. A shaky cakewalk and a funfair with roundabouts. Up and down and round and round they went. There were also stalls selling burgers and pink puff candy. The centre of the Square had been turned into an ice rink and it was crowded with squealing, laughing, woolly-hatted and scarved people whirling around on the ice and having a wonderful time.

The City Chambers was decked out in lights, the towers above spotlit in striking violet and blue.

Music blared out from the fairground, the various rides competing vigorously, causing a discordant clamour that was a constant backdrop to the activities that surrounded Abi.

Excited teenagers queued to get into the ice rink where budding Romeos sought to impress the girls by a combination of skating skills and tomfoolery, under the watchful eyes of the rink attendants. There was a happy buzz of conversation and laughter, punctuated by the occasional tearful outburst as a smaller child was ploughed under by zooming adolescents.

Abi stood for a few minutes watching them all before reluctantly making her way up to the Queen Street Station taxi rank. As usual, she dreaded returning to the empty house, but at this time of year, even more so. She couldn't be bothered sitting down to think of the poems and songs and stories as John had suggested. She couldn't stand being alone much longer. But she doubted if she would have the strength to organise selling up and buying a flat in the city, even if she could bring herself to part with all the memories of Tom that filled the house.

She put on a *CSI: Miami* DVD and collapsed back in her chair with a large glass of brandy.

Horatio, dear, gentle kind Horatio, would keep her company.

22

It wasn't fair, Miss Eden thought. Many shoplifters made it big business and earned more in one day than she earned in a month or more. They came from all over the country to steal and if they got away with it, they stashed their stolen goods in the left luggage offices of Queen Street Station and Central Station and Buchanan Street bus station to be collected later when they were ready to travel back to wherever they'd come from. They even stole to order. They would have shopping lists. Gents' suits, for instance, were a favourite and they stole them in specific sizes. Women's fashion garments were another favourite, and jewellery. Even shoes would be on their lists.

She had got to know quite a few of these shoplifters and had caught them in the act. As a result, they didn't ply their trade in Goodmans so often now. They knew she would be watching their every move. They were also aware that she would have alerted the security guard who would be keeping an eye on them as well.

As it turned out, even the security guards that she had trusted were not above suspicion. One man recently, a very popular and nice man, had really surprised her. His wife was expecting and all the staff in the ground floor departments who knew him best were busy knitting baby clothes. Then on one occasion she had to do a spot check of staff lockers – she had a master key and if goods were going missing it could be part of the procedure to check the lockers. Gents' suits and trousers had been going missing and when she did her search, she found a pair of trousers with the tags and tickets still attached in the security guard's locker. So she took the security guard to the manager's office and he was questioned.

'Oh no, Miss Eden, you've got it all wrong,' he insisted. 'My wife bought those trousers in the Trongate store and they forgot to take the tags off.'

And he stuck to his story. The police were called and the security guard stuck to his story. He was suspended right away and the security company were alerted. He went to court and still said the same. His wife went into the witness box and said she'd bought the trousers, as he'd said, and they hadn't taken the tags off.

Miss Eden might have believed him, indeed wanted to believe him. She found it an ordeal having to stand face to face in court with a man she trusted and liked and felt sorry for. She couldn't believe what he was doing. But someone had seen him selling suits. He knew the days she was in the store and nothing was going missing on those days. He also knew that, if she wasn't in by eleven or twelve, she wasn't coming in that day.

He was duly fined – quite heavily – but wasn't sent to prison because he had no previous convictions. However, he lost his job with the security company and gave himself a bad name. How stupid, Miss Eden thought.

She had spent most of the day in court and then had to write up reports and answer phone calls in her office. As a result, she didn't get a chance to do anything about Mr McKay. She knew without doubt, however, that if she didn't do something very soon, he would end up getting the sack. Despite Mrs Goodman's recent preoccupation with other matters, she was bound to notice Mr McKay any time now and issue him with a written warning.

Goodmans was an excellent place to work, if you were a good worker. The wages couldn't be bettered anywhere. At Christmas, every member of staff, from the youngest junior in the departments and the apprentice joiner and electrician in the basement, received a generous gift. If buyers got married, they were given a wedding present. If a (married) member of staff became pregnant, they were told to choose whatever they wanted or needed from the children's department. If they worked late, they were offered a free meal in the canteen. There was a rest room with a first-aider or nurse in attendance. In other words, the staff had every facility. But if they stepped out of line in any way and were not fulfilling their responsibilities or obligations, Mrs Goodman would be ruthless.

By the time Miss Eden had finished her work, Mr McKay had gone. An assistant manager was left to lock up. This was not supposed to happen. It was, and always had been, Mr McKay's responsibility to lock up. It would have been different if he had been off sick. But he had been in the store all day and had been on duty.

She knew where he would be. Along Argyle Street with the group of tramps, drinking himself unconscious. There was no use confronting him in front of the others. She had to catch him before he got there – either earlier in the shop or as soon as he left the shop and before he had an opportunity to change. She would just have to make time to do that tomorrow.

She discarded the wig and baggy cardigan she had been wearing and changed into her neat navy trouser suit and white blouse. She left the store and walked up Glassford Street. Standing at the traffic lights in Ingram Street, she looked over at the Italian Centre. It was a block of luxury flats, offices and haute couture shops, cafés and classical and contemporary public art. She liked Sandy Stoddart's bronzes of Mercury and

Italia sitting on top of the wall heads. Further along was the imposing Hutchesons' Hall or Hospital. It now belonged to the National Trust for Scotland and attractive, arty things could be bought there. It had been designed originally by two philanthropic brothers to give shelter to the destitute men of Glasgow.

Thinking of destitute men reminded her, perhaps incongruously, of Mr McKay. He wasn't really destitute. He had, she believed, a very respectable villa in Bishopbriggs.

She crossed the road and walked along towards George Square. It was crowded with people strolling around chomping on burgers and fish and chip suppers from one stall and candy floss from another. Others were standing watching the skaters on the specially made ice rink. Long sparkling decorations hung from every lamp-post. Long strands of red lights hung from the high pillar on top of which stood Sir Walter Scott. The whole place had become a temporary fairyland.

Miss Eden loitered for a time to enjoy the antics of the skaters. Some were showing off by swooping and swirling. Others were staggering this way and that before bumping down to a sitting position and laughing helplessly.

She enjoyed watching skating but had never had any inclination to take part. She didn't like to feel helpless in any circumstances. She always liked to feel strong and in charge. Last year, coming home late from the staff Christmas party at Goodmans, she had been set upon by a couple of youths who had tried to rob her. Before they knew what had happened to them, they were flying through the air and crashing to the ground. As soon as they managed to pick themselves up, they ran.

She was glad that tonight was her karate night. It passed an enjoyable couple of hours. She preferred to be active rather than just sit gawping at the television. She read quite a lot of, course, usually in bed before settling down to sleep.

Eventually she made it through the noisy crowds to Queen Street Station and caught the train to Springburn. As the train rocked her gently from side to side, her thoughts turned to Mr McKay again. No doubt he would already be downing Buckfast wine in the dark, dingy cul-de-sac with the group of flea-ridden tramps. It was really dreadful that a smart, efficient, perfectly normal man like Mr McKay should degenerate into such a state, in such a place, and with people like that.

Come what may, tomorrow, she determined, she would do something about Mr McKay. Mr McKay would be tomorrow's priority even if Goodmans was invaded by hordes of shoplifters.

Mr McKay looked worse than ever when she saw him the next morning and she prayed that Mrs Goodman wouldn't see him. If she did come into the store and held the staff meeting, there would be the usual big crowd packed in her office and hopefully Mr McKay would keep to the back out of sight.

In the event, there was a meeting and Miss Eden noticed him slipping into a seat at the back where Mrs Goodman would probably not be able to spot him. She watched him leave the meeting and return to his office. Then he went downstairs to do his usual round of the departments. She slipped into his office, confiscated the plastic shopping bag and took it away to hide it in her own office. That should stop him in his tracks. But she would have to do more than that. He might be so desperate and far gone that he would go drinking with the tramps in his smart suit. Or go drinking anywhere with anyone. It looked as if he was fast becoming an alcoholic.

The day was quite busy. A suspicious-looking woman came in with a big bag and Miss Eden had to watch her and follow her around all the departments, never taking her eyes off her for a second. She saw the woman eventually slip a designer label jacket into the bag. She whispered a warning to the security guard into her mobile phone as she followed the woman towards the front door. Once outside, she stopped the woman and, as expected, she turned nasty and delved into her handbag for a pepperpot. Before she could try to blind Miss Eden with the pepper, however, Miss Eden delivered one of her karate chops. The woman screamed out with pain and fury. It was quite a struggle to get her upstairs to the manager's office. Miss Eden didn't want to risk doing any karate in full view of other customers in the store, so she and the security guard held the woman and helped her along with as little force as they could manage.

Then there was the wait for the police. Even during this time, the woman had to be restrained.

Mr McKay looked grey-faced and on the verge of collapse. By this time, of course, the poor man would have discovered that his bag containing his tramp clothes had gone. He would be feeling confused and anxious. Probably desperate too. He'd be thinking, 'Where has it gone?' and 'What am I going to do?'

After the police had come and gone and the security guard had returned to his post, Miss Eden wondered if this was her chance to speak to Mr McKay and make some sort of move, but decided it would be better to wait until nearer the end of the working day. Perhaps the moment he had locked up, she'd catch him. Yes, best to get the day's work over and both of them safely out of the store. No danger then of being interrupted or found out by any other person in the shop. After all, she did not know how Mr McKay would react. He just wasn't his normal self at all these days.

And so she waited outside but Mr McKay never emerged. She raced round to the back entrance but it too was locked and there was no sign of anyone in the lane. She couldn't understand it. For a time, she searched the nearby streets. She even went to where the tramps and Mr McKay had sat drinking together. The tramps were huddled under pieces of cardboard but there was no sign of Mr McKay. Defeated, she eventually pushed her way through the crowds towards the station. She was no longer interested in watching the skaters or admiring the decorations. She kept thinking about what had happened to Mr McKay. The only answer she could come up with was that he had remained in the store. It seemed ridiculous. Unless, of course, the poor man just couldn't face going home alone to an empty house. He was obviously still devastated over the loss of his wife.

This was a truly terrible state to get into. She'd talk to him tomorrow, first thing. Even if she couldn't catch him on his own, she would ask to speak to him alone in his office. She would say it was urgent and would not take any excuses from him that he was too busy.

Not one more day would pass without her saving him from himself.

23

'For goodness' sake,' Abi burst out irritably, 'a restaurant? What next?'

'Why not?' Douglas Benson asked. 'Every other store has one. Even comparatively small bookshops. I was up in what was Ottakar's bookshop the other day . . .'

'What on earth were you doing there? We have a perfectly good and well-stocked book department here.'

'I was there for research purposes. Waterstone's have bought Ottakar's and it was obviously a very successful takeover. The place was extremely busy.'

'So is our book department.'

'But they have a café with three very attractive girls serving behind the counter, and seats and tables and comfortable arm-chairs and sofas where people can relax with a cup of coffee and browse through the books. It gives a perfect atmosphere and the girls are very attractive. They offer to carry your tray over to the table and ask you if you've enjoyed the coffee or tea or whatever snack you've had to eat.'

He was really getting carried away with enthusiasm.

'The bigger Waterstone's in Sauchiehall Street has a café as well. So does Borders – all very successful businesses.'

Abi sighed. 'In the first place, we are not a bookshop. In the second place, Goodmans is already a very successful business.'

'Yes, but we could be so much more successful. We are so behind the times. It is crazy not to want to expand and modernise and grow . . .'

Abi stopped listening to him. She had heard it all before. But a restaurant of all things! Where on earth would they put it, in the first place? By cutting every other department? She dreaded the thought of what Douglas Benson would do to Goodmans if he had the chance. If only John would take it over. She had made a will leaving everything to him, of course. Perhaps he would employ a suitable managing director or someone who would run the place and keep the old traditions going. Thinking of John made her worries increase. Apparently, the police weren't all that impressed with what John had told them about Julie's ex. Why hadn't he told them before?, they'd asked. She understood why he hadn't, even if the police didn't. John was a very busy man. He had much on his mind. He was recklessly controversial and as a result made a lot of enemies. In other words, he had more to think about than his secretary's ex-boyfriend. She wished with all her heart that John would get out of politics and just come to support her in the store. She could retire then if she knew it was in safe hands. She had been getting so stressed recently, and that was unusual for her. She had been taking more time off than usual too, what with the trip to South Castle-on-Sea and her days in Edinburgh and the times she was persuaded to leave the store during the day before closing time to be with the children. Douglas Benson must be in his element, thinking that he was well on his way to taking over completely.

Remembering South Castle-on-Sea relit the fire of her anger against Mr Webster. To think how lucky he was, with a loving wife and family, and yet he was cheating on them. She had an urge to sack Miss Webster, his daughter, just to spite him, but struggled against the urge. It wasn't his daughter's fault. She was a good worker and had done nothing wrong. It was Mr Webster who deserved to be sacked. She wished she could sack him but knew he was far too valuable an employee. Anyway, sacking from Goodmans wouldn't bother him. He would immediately be snapped up by another firm.

She wondered if she should go to see John again, even just for a chat and to have a bite of lunch. He was always pleased to see her and eager to have a talk with her. He was obviously upset and worried at the moment about the murder. It must be very difficult and stressful for him having to cope with that on top of all his parliamentary work.

'Well,' she suddenly heard Douglas Benson say, 'if that's all at the moment, we'll leave it that I'll enquire further into the possibilities and financial implications for the inclusion of a restaurant or café and report back in due course. Meeting closed.'

Bloody cheek of him! But she couldn't be bothered dragging the meeting out any further. She had too many other things on her mind. As soon as the room cleared, she picked up the phone and dialled John's number. There was no answer. Even if he was in the chamber or elsewhere at a committee meeting or some other engagement, his secretary usually answered and told her where he was. Of course, poor Julie was no longer able to do that. But had he not yet found a replacement?

Surely nothing else had happened? He couldn't be at the police station, could he? Whether or not she could contact him and tell him she was coming didn't matter now. She was so worried, she had to leave for Edinburgh right away.

There was a small space for a taxi rank outside Goodmans – just enough for two taxis. Fortunately there was one taxi waiting there and she climbed in and asked the driver to take her to Queen Street Station. The driver didn't look too pleased but said nothing. She realised Queen Street wasn't much of a job for him and normally she would have walked there. Today, however, she felt so acutely worried and impatient, she didn't feel like struggling through the crowded streets and packed George Square.

The huge Christmas tree and all the lights reminded her of the Christmas family gatherings there used to be in the villa in Huntershill. How wonderful it had been when Tom was alive! The house was a riot of coloured decorations that Tom had spent hours getting ready for the family celebrations. She had always helped him decorate the Christmas tree and they both took great pleasure in wrapping the Christmas gifts.

Now, she just took the family out to a restaurant for lunch. It wasn't the same. In the evening, John usually returned to Edinburgh to have a party in his flat or attend a party in the house of one of the other MSPs. The Bensons usually entertained friends in the evening. They always invited her and, to prevent John worrying, she pretended to go there. But she knew Douglas Benson didn't really want her and she always made some last-minute excuse.

On Christmas Eve, though, she always had some fun when she visited the children. But no matter what she did or didn't do, Christmas was no longer a happy family time for her. New Year was even worse. She told John and the Bensons that she would be going away for a few days. Sometimes she did go away to some hotel or other. A lot of people spent Hogmanay (New Year's Eve) and New Year's Day and the day after in a hotel. It didn't matter what she did, however. It was still a painful and unhappy time. And there was always the silent, empty house to come back to.

She did not have to wait for a train and boarded one just minutes before it moved off.

Most evenings, whether it was during the year or at holiday time, she just watched television. If there was no programme that she liked, she would put on one of her *CSI: Miami* DVDs and take some pleasure and comfort from Horatio, the way he bent forward, head leaning to one side as he listened with concentration, sympathy and understanding to whoever was in need of sympathy and understanding. Often he would say to a helpless child or a woman who had been hurt or frightened, 'No one is going to hurt you ever again. Trust me.'

Usually the train seemed to fly towards Edinburgh, but today it felt as if it would never get there. She bought a cup of tea from the trolley and a packet of biscuits. She hadn't bothered to make any breakfast before leaving for the store in the morning. She tried John's number on her mobile. Still no reply.

She decided to call at his flat first just in case he was there. There was no answer to her insistent ringing of his doorbell. She walked from there down the Royal Mile to the Parliament. At the counter where visitors booked tours or made enquiries, she asked the girl to contact John's office and tell him that his mother was here.

'I'm sorry,' the girl said eventually, 'he appears to be visiting his constituency today. Would you like to leave a message? He'll probably be speaking at meetings there and when he's doing that, he turns off his mobile.'

'No, I'll phone him tomorrow, or later this evening.'

She turned away, almost in tears with disappointment but hardening it away with annoyance. What a waste of time – coming all this distance for nothing. She might as well make a few purchases on her way back to the station.

She had a walk around the Grassmarket and looked at the boutiques. She stopped also to look at the railed enclosure that marked the site of the gallows. Captain Porteous was hanged there and over a hundred Covenanters were martyred. Not far away was the house where Burke and Hare, the bodysnatchers and murderers, operated.

Edinburgh had a fascinating history and a bloody one, of course. It had been a legal and middle- and upper-class city, whereas Glasgow had been basically industrial and working-class with its shipbuilding and locomotive works and other industries. The patron saint of Glasgow was Saint Kentigern – or Mungo as Glaswegians preferred to call him. Mungo meant 'dear one'. The city had its very beginnings rooted in religion.

By the end of the fifteenth century, Glasgow was a powerful academic and ecclesiastical centre. Then by 1770, trade with America was fully established. Glasgow's tobacco lords had cornered the market.

Abi admired the hard-working, inventive and friendly people of Glasgow. She admired the city of Edinburgh in many ways, and enjoyed a day's visit to the capital, but she would never want to live there. To her, it would feel like living among strangers in a foreign country.

As soon as people who lived in the Royal Mile became successful, they moved away to the New Town. It was very elegant and designed by Robert Adam. Abi still preferred Glasgow's Victorian architecture, though. John always laughed at her for the way she kept sticking up for Glasgow and everything about it, no matter what.

'Well,' she said, 'I'm Glasgow born and bred, and proud of it.'

John had been born and bred in Glasgow too, of course, but he preferred living in Edinburgh and had been perfectly happy in the capital – until now. She wished she'd seen him today and found out how he was and if there had been any further developments in the murder enquiries. She had lunch in Jenners in Princes Street and then caught a train back to Glasgow. Once in Queen Street Station, she hesitated about going straight home or returning to the store, but it would soon be closing time. It was hardly worth it. She made her way down to George Square, not sure what she was going to do, but reluctant to return to Huntershill.

The Square was teeming with people as usual at this time

of year and was all raucous noise and sparkle. She stood for a time watching the skaters, then decided that now that she was so near, she might as well pay a visit to the penthouse and say hello to the children.

It was Douglas who answered the door and to her surprise, he was quite chatty and welcoming to her. He even called her 'Mother'. But of course, when she came to think about it, he was happy because he thought he was winning. He believed he was on the verge of taking over completely. She had been so lax recently. She must try and pull herself together and get back to her old routine. She must get back her concentration on the store and everyone in it. She hadn't even seen Mr McKay for days, weeks maybe. She couldn't remember. That was the worrying thing. She probably had seen him, spoken to him too, but her mind was just not on the job.

She would try to get a decent sleep tonight and go into the store tomorrow with a fresh mind and a renewal of her steely determination to run the store her way, Tom's way, the way it had always been run.

24

'I'm telling you, Moira,' Sam Webster said, 'she's stalking me. She came to the shop and I told her to fuck off. But she hung on and so I took her to the station. I meant to wait and put her on a train to South Castle-on-Sea but there wasn't a train due for hours and so I left her there to catch the train herself. I didn't want to sit there with her for all that time. Or any time. I just wanted rid of the bloody awful woman.'

'Well, you haven't got rid of her.'

It was then that they heard a crash and ran through to the kitchen. A brick had been hurled through the window. Glass lay scattered over the units and the floor.

Sam Webster tore open the back door and rushed outside but there was no one to be seen. He returned, cursing under his breath.

'Don't tell me that was her back,' Moira said.

'Who else?'

'If this goes on, we'll have to phone for the police. There was one of the garden ornaments broken yesterday. That was probably her as well.'

'I'll threaten her with the police if I see her tomorrow. But I don't want the police involved if I can help it. Apart from anything else, there's my job to consider.'

'You should have thought about that before you became involved with her.'

'I wish I'd never set eyes on the woman. The only thing I can think of is to let her know that if I see her in the shop again, I'm going back down to South Castle-on-Sea. Then I could perhaps involve the police down there, or threaten to involve the police and the local paper. That would risk her B. & B. going down the drain. She wouldn't want that.'

Moira shrugged. 'I suppose you'll be going anyway.'

'Well, I need to be there on business, but don't worry, last time I was in a hotel at the other end of South Castle-on-Sea from her B. & B. and will be every time from now on.'

The more he thought about it, the more he was sure that this was the best idea. The Floral was Viv's livelihood and she was proud of the place. She would definitely not want it involved in any scandal. Families with young children were among her best customers because of The Floral's closeness to the beach and the pier, with all its entertainments. If Viv was proved to be a bad and dangerous character, no family would want to go near her.

Next day, like the last few days, Viv was loitering near the entrance of the shop. He went straight over to her and said, 'Look, you may as well give up hanging around here. I'm off to South Castle-on-Sea to see my wholesalers later today. So I won't be here for you to pester.'

Then he went into the store and upstairs to report to Mrs Goodman. Or Benson if Mrs Goodman wasn't around. He didn't know what was up with her recently. You could never depend on where she was or what she was doing. It wasn't like her. Maybe she was getting too old for the job. She must be close to sixty by now.

After making some phone calls and collecting some papers and his order book, he returned outside and picked up his car from the multi-storey car park. There was no sign of Viv. No doubt she would be away to the station to find out about the quickest train to South Castle-on-Sea.

It was too bad that it hadn't been the summer season. She would have been tied to The Floral and not able to travel around pestering him. It was just his bad luck it had all blown up during the winter when she'd nothing better to do.

He tried to put her out of his mind as he drove down south. He concentrated on his driving. Or at least he tried to. But every now and again, she would intrude into his thoughts again. Even when he thought about plans for Christmas. He simply must get the problem of Viv solved once and for all during this visit to South Castle-on-Sea. She must not be allowed to control and spoil his and his family's Christmas. They always had such a happy time. The girls were at home and the house was always beautifully decorated. The Christmas tree in the corner of the sitting room sparkled with light and there were presents piled at the foot of it. They had Christmas lunch as a family, but in the evening friends arrived for a Christmas party with everyone raising their champagne glasses and wishing each other a merry Christmas. Then there would be the other happy celebrations at New Year when they visited friends.

No way was he going to allow Viv to spoil all that. What on earth did she think she would get out of it? Did she actually believe that she would get him to go back and sleep with her at her B. & B.?

No, it was surely just badness and malice and a determination for revenge. Why hadn't he seen she was a woman like that right from the start? He cursed himself for being such a gullible idiot.

Once in South Castle-on-Sea, he went straight to The Floral and banged on the door. There was no reply and the front windows were in darkness. He went round the back. Darkness again. Nevertheless, he thumped his fist against the back door. No reply. If she had been in, she would have opened the door. She would not have missed a chance of speaking to him and probably trying to entice him in. The only thing he could think of was that she had missed the train and hadn't yet arrived in South Castle-on-Sea.

He decided to attend to business and then come back to The Floral later.

He saw his inventor first and then one of the wholesalers. After that, he went back to The Floral and tried the doors again. Still nothing. He had got back into his car and was sitting wondering whether to wait there or go for something to eat, when his mobile rang. It was Moira, in obvious distress.

'Darling, what's wrong?'

She started to sob so much, she couldn't speak for what seemed an eternity.

'Moira, for God's sake, what's happened?'

'The house is on fire. The fire brigade are trying to put the fire out but it's too late. Everything's up in flames. Everything's gone.'

'Are you and the girls all right?' he shouted back in panic.

'Yes, thank God, we were along the road visiting the Davidsons. We saw the flames from there and phoned the fire brigade and the police. I've told the police about her. It could only be your madwoman who's done this. I've told the police everything. You obviously hadn't the guts to do it.'

'Moira!' He was heartbroken. 'You did the right thing, darling. I'm on my way. I'll be with you as soon as I can.'

He tossed the phone aside, put his foot down and the car shot forward into the darkness. He could have wept. His whole life was shattered. He would have told the Glasgow police himself, only he had believed that the threat of reporting her behaviour to the police in South Castle-on-Sea and the local paper there would have been enough to stop Viv. She would have known that such publicity would have ruined her business. She would have given up as a result and left him and his family in peace. They would still have had their home. He would still have had his job. Now, if there was publicity in Glasgow about what had happened, he was sure of nothing. Except that he had been the root cause of everything. If he hadn't met Viv, if he hadn't slept with her, nothing else would have happened. God knows what she would say now. Probably she would claim that he had seduced her, forced her against her will, raped her, and ruined her reputation. He shuddered to think what lies her twisted mind would think up. There was no telling what she'd do or say, what she'd be capable of. The woman was mad.

There would have been no use waiting to speak to her, even if she'd escaped the police in Glasgow and was on her way to South Castle-on-Sea. Speaking to her, he realised now, would just have made matters worse. The tears were escaping now. He blinked them away so that he could see to drive home. Only this time he had no home to return to.

As soon as he got back to Glasgow, and then to Bearsden, the first thing he saw was the police standing outside the burnt-out shell of the house, and a tape stretched across the garden with the words 'Crime Scene'. He drove further along to the Davidsons' house and although it was the very early hours of the morning, he jumped out of his car and knocked loudly on the door. It was opened by Mrs Davidson wearing a white dressing gown. She stood aside to let him enter, saying, 'The girls are in bed in the spare room but Moira wouldn't go to bed. Hardly worthwhile, right enough. We've all been up half the night. She's lying down on the settee in the sitting room.'

He strode across the hall and into the sitting room. A tear-stained Moira rose up from the settee and he rushed over to gather her into his arms.

'Oh, Moira.'

He held her close and she sobbed out the words, 'She tossed aside the petrol can she used and the police got fingerprints. I saw her hanging about earlier and gave them her description. They picked her up at the railway station, in the waiting room.'

'Well, thank God for that. At least she won't be tormenting us any more.'

'What are we going to do?'

'I'll book us into a hotel in town until we can organise something more permanent. Has everything in the house gone?'

She shook her head. 'Probably. I don't know. I can't bear to look.'

'I'll see to that. Don't worry. We'll get over this.'

Mrs Davidson came into the room then, carrying a tray on which was a pot of tea and a plate of warm croissants. She set it down on a coffee table and poured a cup of tea for each of them. She said, 'The fire brigade are not long gone. Everything's safe now apparently. The fire is completely out, thank goodness. At one point, I was afraid it was going to spread.'

Moira drank her tea and dried her eyes.

'She's mad. Just as you said. Completely mad.'

'Try not to think about it, darling. After I drink this tea, I'll go along and have a look and see if I can salvage anything. That's if the police will allow me at this stage. But if necessary, I'll hire a van or whatever. I'll also book us into a hotel.'

'You're welcome to stay here,' Mrs Davidson said. 'I can always make up a bed for the pair of you in here.'

'No, no,' Sam said. 'You've been kind enough as it is and we're more than grateful. If you could just look after my wife and daughters until I come back from town and have everything organised, that would be a help.'

'Of course. Take as much time as you need.'

He gave Moira another hug and said, 'I'll be as quick as I can.' Then he hurried away. He spoke to one of the policemen still on guard in front of the house, before looking around. He could see that there were some things he could salvage, but that job would have to wait till the police were finished with their investigations. He drove from Bearsden into town and parked his car near the store. After checking with a few hotels, he managed to get a booking in the Millennium Hotel in George Square. There had been a last-minute cancellation and he was lucky he had arrived just at the right time. Lucky indeed, because it was a good hotel right next to the train station and not far from the store. Fronting the Square, the hotel had a large glass conservatory area where customers and residents could sit and watch everything that was going on in the square while drinking tea or coffee, or something stronger. And there was certainly plenty going on in the Square at the moment. He prayed it would help even in a small way to distract his family's attentions from their troubles.

He hurried across the Square, skirting the ice rink and the Christmas tree, and then crossed the road towards Glassford Street. The store was not yet open and so he went and sat in his car until Mr McKay arrived and unlocked the front doors.

He was taken aback by Mr McKay's appearance. He looked a different man. However, he was too taken up with his own problems to think about any Mr McKay might have. He had to go up to his office and get a few things sorted out, while waiting for Mrs Goodman to arrive. Then he would have to confess everything to her. Tell her the exact truth. The truth, the whole truth, and nothing but the truth. He'd apologise and say he'd have to take at least a couple of days off to settle his family in the hotel and to see if and when he could salvage anything from the wreck that had once been his home. He would also have to bring his family over to Goodmans to purchase clothes and whatever they needed while they were living in the hotel.

He had no idea what Mrs Goodman's reaction would be but it was better if everything came from him, rather than have her read about it in the newspapers.

Whatever her reaction would be, he had to face it.

He braced himself.

25

By the time Miss Eden got upstairs, she had missed Mr McKay. No doubt he was already doing his usual round of the departments. She went into his office and immediately saw a sleeping bag lying on the floor. He must have taken it from the bedding department and slept in his office overnight. She groaned to herself. This obviously could not go on.

He had only reached the furniture department on the third floor when she found him. 'Mr McKay, I need to have a private word right away. Can we go back upstairs to your office? Now,' she added firmly.

He looked confused and she cupped his elbow in one hand and steered him towards the stairs.

'This is not a good time, Miss Eden,' he managed. 'I'm very busy.'

She did not loosen her grip and they continued up the stairs and along the corridor to his office.

'Really, Miss Eden,' he protested, and tried to stop in his tracks outside the office door.

She opened it and forced him inside. She shut the door and faced him. 'You cannot go on like this, Mr McKay. You're liable to get the sack any day now. It's a miracle you haven't already been dismissed.'

'I don't know what you're talking about.'

'Yes, you do. I'm not a detective for nothing. I know all about you changing into shabby clothes and drinking with tramps. Drinking yourself silly. You're well on the way to becoming an alcoholic and ruining your whole life. It must stop before anyone else finds out.'

To her acute embarrassment, he suddenly began to shake violently and sob.

'Now, now.' She tried to sound comforting. She patted his back. 'I'll help you. You're going to be all right.'

'How can I be? I can't bear to go home. I can't face life . . . I haven't got any life without Jenny. I need a drink.'

'No, you don't.' She hesitated, and then said, 'You'll come home with me until we get you properly over this. I've got a spare room. You'll be safe and comfortable and you won't be alone in the house. You'll stay in my house until you get off drinking and are back to your old self again. I'll help you. I'm going to make sure that you get over this and are strong and in charge of yourself again.'

He mopped his face with a handkerchief. 'It's no use, Miss Eden. It's kind of you but you don't understand . . .'

'Mr McKay, give me your house keys. I'll go over to your place right now and collect all you need. Your clothes and toilet gear and so on. Come on now. You're going to get over this. It'll just take a little time. Give me your keys.'

He groped in his pocket and came out with a keyring.

'Thank you. Now, instead of going around the departments, stay here and catch up on some phone calls and paperwork. I'll go and fill a suitcase with your things and take it to my flat. Then I'll come back on duty. After you lock up, I'll take you home with me to Springburn.'

He stared at her helplessly.

'Come on.' She steered him over to his desk. 'Concentrate on some paperwork. Everything's going to be all right. Believe me, it'll just take a little time.'

She hoped she was right. He looked as if he needed a doctor or a psychiatrist. Or both. However, she couldn't just let the man ruin his life as he was doing. Fancy Mr McKay – Mr McKay of all people – drinking himself unconscious with a crowd of tramps. Unable to do his job properly. Actually dossing down overnight in the store. Mr McKay had always been so conscientious and correct. An excellent and well-respected manager.

It just couldn't be allowed to go on. Her solution seemed the only way. It certainly was the only way she could think of. It was with some frustration and impatience, however, that she made her way to Bishopbriggs. She could have done without a lodger, especially at this time of year. It was such an intrusion on her freedom and her comfortable routine. Tonight, for instance, was one of her karate nights. It was something she always enjoyed. It was important too that she kept fit and strong and efficient. That meant plenty of practice at karate. But of course, she daren't leave Mr McKay alone in the house. Especially not on his first night. She got off the train at Bishopbriggs Station, and found she had quite a long walk through the main shopping area and beyond to reach Mr McKay's villa. Inside, she was shocked at what she found. The place was littered with papers, clothes, empty wine bottles, dirty dishes and stale food.

She began the job of cleaning up as best as she could. She filled a bin bag with the rubbish and bottles, washed the dishes in the kitchen sink and hoovered the carpet. Then she searched through the wardrobe and cupboards, found a large suitcase and filled it with a suit, shirts, socks, underwear, shoes, a hat, a pair of gloves, a couple of pairs of pyjamas, a dressing gown, a coat, shaving gear and other toilet goods. Then she phoned for a taxi to take her to her flat. She would have been strong enough to carry the heavy case all the way back to the station, but she still had hours of work ahead of her and she had been off duty long enough already.

Thinking of strength and her karate made her remember a recent charity event she'd taken part in. It was for a children's hospice to fund a party for the children and give them Christmas presents. One of the things she'd done was to break a pile of roof slates in two with one blow from the side of her hand. Another had been jumping, spinning back and kicking a pad. Quite a sum of money had been raised.

Once she reached her flat, she took Mr McKay's case into the spare bedroom and unpacked it into empty drawers and a wardrobe. Then she fetched bed linen and blankets from the linen cupboard and made up the bed.

At last, everything organised, she went across the road to the station and caught a train going to Queen Street. George Square was busy but no doubt would get even busier once darkness fell and everything was lit up. Glancing at her watch, she hurried across the Square, down South Frederick Street to Ingram Street, then round to Glassford Street. She hoped Mr McKay had remained in his office and that Mrs Goodman had not seen him. And that no one else had seen him. He looked such a shabby wreck of a man.

On the way up to his office, she was stopped in her tracks by a woman going into the fitting room in Fashions. There wasn't an assistant anywhere around. Annoyance made her shake her head in disbelief. She had lost count of the times she had told assistants always to watch anyone who went into a fitting room, and to check all garments that were taken in by customers.

The customer had disappeared into the fitting room carrying a pile of garments over one arm and a large shopping bag over the other. It was impossible to tell how many garments there were. Miss Eden loitered nearby, pretending she was examining some jackets. Eventually the woman reappeared and walked away towards the lift. What a bloody cheek, Miss Eden thought. Usually a fitting room thief would return some of the garments and just leave with one or perhaps two stolen items. She followed the woman into the lift and stood silently beside her as it plummeted down to the ground floor. Then, at a discreet distance, she whispered into her mobile. As a result, the security guard was waiting watchfully at the front door. As soon as the woman left the store, both Miss Eden and the security guard stood in front of her and Miss Eden said, 'I have reason to believe you are carrying goods from the store that you haven't paid for. I'd like you to accompany me to the manager's office.'

The woman turned quietly back towards the front door. Then suddenly, unexpectedly, she started to race along Glassford Street. In a matter of seconds, Miss Eden had caught her, grabbed her elbow, and swung her back round towards the store.

'The manager's office, I said.'

Mr McKay was in his office and he quickly agreed to phone for the police after the woman's shopping bag revealed several fashion garments which she hadn't paid for. The usual routine was adhered to, and it seemed to take an age. Miss Eden was impatient, indeed anxious, for closing time to arrive so that she could get Mr McKay safely away to Springburn. At last he was locking up the front and back doors, and they were then on their way up to Queen Street. Mr McKay was silent until they were near the station.

'Miss Eden, I really think I should just go to Bishopbriggs. From what you've told me, you've made the place habitable again. It's really very kind of you but I believe I'll be all right now, so . . .'

'No, you will not, Mr McKay. You need time away from being alone in your house, and you need help to stop your drinking. As soon as my back was turned, you'd be back downing Buckie with those tramps.'

'Really, Miss Eden . . .' He tried to sound insulted and angry, but failed. He allowed himself to be hustled onto the train, then off again at Springburn.

'Just across the road here,' Miss Eden said. 'Springburn used to be a really nice and friendly community, and a good shopping centre, but now it has no heart.' She shook her head. 'I remember the Co-op and Hoey's. A whole line of good shops where you could buy absolutely everything. You never needed to go into town.'

Cupping his elbow in one hand, she guided Mr McKay up the stairs.

'Here we are.' She opened the door. 'Welcome to my humble abode.'

'Thank you,' Mr McKay said faintly.

'I had central heating put in so it's nice and cosy. Just go into the kitchen. I've a wee dining table and some chairs there. And everything's fitted.'

Mr McKay looked somewhat dazedly around the small kitchen.

'It's very nice.'

'And cosy.'

'Yes, and cosy.'

'See where the table and chairs are? That used to be a hole in the wall bed.'

'A hole in the wall . . .?'

'Yes, that's what a bed recess was called.'

'Oh.'

'But there's two bedrooms and a sitting room and so I didn't need a bed in here as well. It's far more useful as a dining area. Don't you think?'

'Oh, indeed.'

'I'll put the kettle on. I've got a steak pie and mashed

165

potatoes ready just to heat up in the micro. Is that all right for you?'

'Yes, thank you. It's very kind of you, Miss Eden.'

'So you keep telling me. Just forget it. You're a good manager and you're needed at the store. It's the least I can do. After all, the store has been good to us.'

'Oh, indeed.'

'Just sit down and relax.' She put the food in the microwave oven and set the table. Then she said, 'Come on through and I'll show you your room and where I've put all your things.' She also showed him where the bathroom was situated off the hall. Once they were back in the kitchen and she had dished up the meal, Mr McKay said, 'That's part of my trouble.'

'What is?'

'The store has been so good to me and . . .' He hesitated and looked in danger of bursting into tears. 'That money . . . all that money lost to the firm because of me. It was terrible what . . .'

'Stop right there. The store is well insured and so they haven't suffered one jot. They haven't lost anything and it's not a trouble for them. You really must, I said *must*, forget about that, Mr McKay. You must put it out of your mind. It's in the past. Nobody has suffered because of it but yourself. You've obviously suffered mentally as well as physically. It's time you stopped suffering. From this moment on, you have never to think of that incident ever again. Do you hear me, Mr McKay?'

'But you see . . .'

'Stop it, Mr McKay. What good do you think you're doing to yourself or anyone else carrying on the way you are? What you need to do is get back to being the excellent manager you always were for the store and for Mrs Goodman. That's all she needs and wants – she needs and wants you to keep the store in good order and flourishing. Is that pie all right for you?'

'Oh yes, indeed. Very tasty.'

'Right, wire in, as my mother used to say.'

Mr McKay managed a weak smile. 'That's a very old Scottish expression. I remember my mother saying that as well.'

'There you are then. Now, afterwards, will we sit and chat or watch television? We could watch the news and then have a chat about all that's been happening in the store. How's that? Will that be all right?'

'Oh yes, indeed,' Mr McKay said.

26

'Oh, you didn't, John!'

'There's no need to look so shocked, Mum. I can afford it.'

'But a reward? Isn't it the police who are supposed to do that?'

John shrugged. 'I've no idea. But anyway, I thought it might help if I put up a reward for any information that would lead to the arrest of the murderer. Also, I gave as good a description as I could of Julie's ex-boyfriend and asked if he would come forward to help the police with their enquiries. Or if anyone knew of his whereabouts.'

'Oh dear, I hope the police won't be angry with you. You probably should have consulted them first.'

He shrugged again. 'Well, it's all over the newspapers now so there's nothing much they can do about it. But they should be pleased. The chances are it'll help them find the killer.'

Another thought struck Abi, a much more worrying thought. 'Oh, John, what if it makes that man angry at you – Julie's ex? And what if he is a murderer? He might come after you.'

'Och, what would he want with me?'

'If he was angry at you for giving his description. And if he is the killer, he must be mad and so there's no telling what he might do.'

John laughed. 'Well, thanks very much, Mum. You're a great comfort to me.'

'I can't help worrying about you.'

'I'll be fine.'

'In that flat on your own at night as well.'

'Mum, stop it. I'm not a child any more. I can look after myself.'

'Do you think I should come through and stay with you for a while?'

He laughed again. 'Oh, right. You'd be a great protection. Anyway, I work late here in the Parliament most nights. Or I'm travelling round the constituency on business. So it would just mean you'd be alone in the flat most of the time.'

Abi finished her cup of tea.

'Well, you take care, do you hear?'

'Yes, Mother.'

'I'd better get back. Douglas is enjoying himself these days. He thinks I'm well on my way to giving up the store. I haven't been paying much attention to it recently, what with one thing and another. That's the only reason he encourages me to visit the children so often. If he gets the store, he wouldn't care if I never saw the children.'

'They're your grandchildren. You're entitled to see them as often as you like. Will you be calling in there tonight?' He glanced at his watch. 'It's not worth your while going back to work now.'

'I know, and of course their house is on my way home. I mean, being just down from the station. And I do enjoy seeing them and making them laugh with all my nonsense songs and poems and all the stories I make up.'

'Have you done anything yet about putting them together in a book?'

She shook her head.

'Who would want to publish a book like that?'

'A Scottish publisher, I keep telling you. And I've heard there's some millionaire entrepreneur bought over one small Scottish firm. But there's quite a few others. I'll make a list out for you. You can try them all if necessary. I'm sure some Scottish publisher would be interested.'

'Oh well, I'll think about it.'

'You said that before. Get down to it, Mum. It would give you something to do at night. It would be a good cheery way to pass your time.'

'Yes, all right, dear.'

'Promise me you'll do it.'

'I promise.'

She supposed he was right. At least it would give her something to do during the long dark winter nights. That was the only drawback about having concentrated every moment of her life on the store and on Tom in and out of the store. She had never been one for socialising at the best of times, and as a result, she had never really made any friends. Now she had noticed that even John had begun to think that working in the store was getting too much for her. Or was it her over-sensitive imagination? One thing was sure, he had begun to agree with her that there was no use clinging on to the past in the house in Huntershill.

'It's not good for you to be there on your own, Mum, especially during the long winter nights. It might be a good idea to sell the house and buy a flat in town. It's not doing you any good clinging on to the past so much. It's making you depressed.'

The next thing would be the store.

'No use clinging on to the past in the store, Mum. We'll have to face it. Times change . . .' He hadn't said it yet. Mainly, she suspected, because he hated Douglas Benson. But she was afraid he would say it one day.

Even he could see that she hadn't the same interest in

working in the store as she used to. Her heart wasn't really in it since Tom was no longer there. There were so many worries in connection with it now. The latest thing was Mr Webster, who had come to her and told her such a hair-raising story. She couldn't help feeling sorry for him. Well, not so much for him, perhaps, but certainly for his family. She'd seen the day when she would not have felt in the least sorry. She would just have thought he'd brought it all on himself. Indeed, she would have told him so. Instead she had listened patiently and thought about how upset his wife and daughters must be, seeing their home go up in flames. She was thinking, of course, of her own home and what she would feel about losing it.

She ended up telling Mr Webster to take as much time off as he needed to find a new house, and she suggested the convenience of the Italian Centre or the big flats in the new conversion further along Ingram Street. No doubt she noticed these places because they had been at the back of her mind for herself.

Mr Webster was nearly in tears of gratitude. She had thought for a moment that he was going to embrace her.

'Get back to your family and tell them everything's going to be all right,' she said abruptly and he turned away and left the office.

She sat at home that night, her mind still swirling with problems, other people's as well as her own. Especially John's, of course. She felt haunted by apprehension. She couldn't bear the thought that he might be in danger.

She tried her best to do as he had told her and concentrate on writing down the wee songs that made the children laugh and at one time had made her laugh too.

Twelve an' a tanner a bottle,
That's what it's costin' today.

Twelve an' a tanner a bottle,
Takes aw the pleasure away.
For if you want a wee drappie,
You've got to spend aw that you've got.
How can a fella be happy,
When happiness costs such a lot?

She flung down her pen. It was no use. She couldn't continue writing. She wanted to phone John but he'd told her he'd be talking at a meeting in his constituency and she didn't know what hotel he'd be staying in. She felt in such an agony of fear that she had to take a sleeping pill to knock her out.

Next day, on her way to work, she saw the headlines on a billboard and bought a newspaper. It turned out that Julie's ex had come forward immediately and told the police he had been at the birthday party of his fiancée's mother on the evening of the murder. The party had gone on quite late and he had been invited to stay the night. In other words, the man, who seemed a decent sort, was happily engaged to be married and had a watertight alibi.

So much for all the apprehension and fear she had been suffering. It just showed what stress she was under, what with the situation at the store with Douglas Benson and not being able to cope with her grief at being without Tom, and the thought of perhaps having to give up the home they had shared and loved so much. But if she did give up working in the store, and if she did sell the house, what would she do with her life? It was all very well talking about giving up the past and looking to the future, but what future? She couldn't see much of a future in writing that book of songs and poems. Now that she'd started it, she probably would continue with it just to please John, but that wouldn't take very long.

She took a deep breath as she entered the store. She said

her usual polite good mornings to everyone as she passed to get the lift up to her office. She must hang on to the store for as long as she was able. But meantime, she would try to summon enough courage to sell the house, leave Huntershill, and look for a flat in town. At least that way, she would save a bit of energy travelling to and fro and so she might feel more physically able to carry on at work.

Benson asked her about Mr Webster and was obviously annoyed that she had dealt with him, and about the way she had dealt with him.

'Why didn't you sack him?'

'Why should I have sacked him?'

'Why?' Benson rolled his eyes. 'Because he's caused the store so much bloody bad publicity, of course.'

'I'm quite sure Mr Webster's private life will not affect Goodmans' sales figures one iota.'

'I certainly hope you're right.'

'I know the business and what would affect it and what would not.'

'Oh well,' he sounded sarcastic, 'that's all right then.'

Abi raised an eyebrow. 'Was there anything else?'

He turned and stormed out of the office, banging the door shut behind him.

Abi decided it would be better not to visit the children after work. She didn't feel like facing a glowering son-in-law again that day. She reluctantly returned to Huntershill and switched on all the lights and the television in an effort to make the place look cheerful and to give an illusion of company.

Later she did a bit more writing.

There is a happy land in Duke Street jail
Where all the prisoners get their dinner in a pail.
Oh, how they shout and yell when they hear the dinner bell,
Then the shouts turn to dismay – It's mince again today!

27

'Of course we must have decorations,' Miss Eden said. 'It's Christmas. We'll have a tree as well but just a miniature one. Just as a token.'

She unravelled a pile of coloured paper chains.

'I'll drape them on the walls. You hold the ladder and pass them up to me. We'll just have them in here because we spend more time in the kitchen. And maybe a couple in the hall would look nice and welcoming.'

There were glistening gold and silver shapes as well.

'The store is beautifully decorated, isn't it?'

'Yes,' Mr McKay agreed. 'I believe the staff surpassed themselves this year.'

'Yes, it wasn't just the joiners and some of the other men from the basement with their ladders. The girls in the departments did their bit. I liked the way they draped decorations along the front of the counters and around the glass cases. The place looked really cheery and Christmassy.'

'Indeed. A riot of colour.'

'Did you have a look in the toy department?'

'Of course.'

'I thought it was lovely to see the children's faces when they met Santa. Who was it this year, by the way?'

'Mr Campbell from Men's Underwear.'

'That was a good choice. He wouldn't need any padding.'

It was the first time since Mr McKay had become her lodger that she had seen him smile. It was only a small smile, but all the same, it was progress. He handed up some decorations.

'Last year, if you remember,' he said, 'it was Mr Webster because he was so big. Nevertheless, he needed padding to make him look suitably rotund. This year, his image has become tarnished. Although, of course, the children will not be aware of that.'

'Oh well, it's the temptation of the job. I mean, being away from his home and his wife so much . . .'

'I would never have been unfaithful to Jenny. Never, no matter how often we were separated.'

'You were never tested, though, Mr McKay. Not like Mr Webster. I'm sure he loves his wife . . .'

'I'd never, never,' Mr McKay repeated with much feeling, 'have been unfaithful to Jenny. No matter how often or how far away from her I had to go.'

'All right, all right,' Miss Eden soothed. 'I believe you, Mr McKay. Now how about a gold one over the fireplace?' And in the dining alcove? As I think I told you, that used to be what was known as a hole in the wall bed. But everyone has had the beds taken out and a table and chairs put in there instead. Or at least everyone I know of.'

'Really?'

'Oh yes, and at one time there would have been a coal bunker in here, in everyone's kitchen, and the coalman would have trudged up the stairs with a bag of coal on his back and emptied the coal into the bunker. Think of all the dust the coal would make. And in a place where people cooked and ate.'

'Most unhealthy.'

'Yes, I don't think that would be allowed these days. Think

of all the health and safety rules there are in the store. And the only cooking that's done there – and very little at that – is in the canteen.'

'Of course the canteen is very modern compared with the rest of the store. It had to be brought up to modern standards.'

'That's true. Now how does that look?'

Miss Eden stood back to admire the room.

'Very festive. Very festive indeed, Miss Eden.'

'Now, I must ask you a favour, Mr McKay. This is one of my karate nights. I'm a member of a local karate club. I enjoy it and it keeps me fit and strong. But I don't want to leave you in the house alone. At the same time, I don't like missing my club. I've already missed more than one evening since you've been here.'

'Oh, I'm so sorry, Miss Eden. Of course you must go this evening and not worry about me.'

'No, no. In my opinion, you're not well enough to be left alone yet, Mr McKay. The alternative is for you to come with me. You might find it interesting to sit and watch all the members perform. You might be surprised to see what I can do. I mean, I'm not very tall, as you can see, and I'm quite slim, but I can throw a big, heavily built man, no bother.'

'Oh, I don't know if I . . .'

'Yes, you must come. If you don't, it means that I won't go either. Do it as a favour for me, Mr McKay. After all, I'm doing my best for you.'

After a few moments of unhappy hesitation, Mr McKay said, 'Very well, Miss Eden. But I cannot take part.'

Miss Eden laughed. 'Definitely not, Mr McKay. Don't worry about that. You'll get a nice cup of tea and you'll sit well away from the action but be able to watch it while you enjoy your tea. As I say, you might find it interesting, enjoyable even.'

And so, after the surplus decorations were tidied away and Mr McKay had carried the stepladder back to the hall cupboard, they set off for the community centre where the local karate club met.

On the way back home, Miss Eden said, 'Well, did you enjoy it? Or at least find it interesting, Mr McKay?'

Mr McKay actually gave quite a big smile. 'Oh yes, Miss Eden, both enjoyable and very interesting. Yes indeed. I never imagined you capable of . . . You always seemed quite delicate in a way. I mean, you're so slim and neat and you obviously never behave like that in the store. To see you jumping around and kicking and throwing people about . . .' He almost laughed. 'Quite amazing. And so this is your hobby? This is what you do in your spare time?'

'Yes. I've been a member of the club for years. As I say, it keeps me fit and I enjoy it. You'll come again, won't you?'

'If you wish me to.'

'I definitely don't want to leave you in the house on your own.'

'Very well.'

They'd had dinner earlier when they'd arrived home from the shop but now Miss Eden made a light supper because karate always gave her an appetite. They sat on either side of the fire enjoying scrambled eggs on a roll and a cup of tea.

It had been agreed that Mr McKay would have his bath in the evening and she would have hers in the morning and so, after watching the news on television, Mr McKay said, 'Let me help you with the dishes and setting the breakfast table before I have my bath.'

'All right. You wash and dry the dishes and I'll set the table.'

It saved time in the morning if the breakfast table was set ready.

'Would you like a hot water bottle, Mr McKay? I've got two so there's no problem and it's a very cold night.'

'Very well.'

She filled the kettle and brought out two rubber bottles from a cupboard.

'Bacon and fried egg all right for breakfast?'

'Yes, indeed.'

Miss Eden thought how pleasant it was to have company in the house. She hadn't relished the thought of a lodger at first, especially if it meant missing her karate club, but everything was beginning to work out quite well. And of course, she had the added satisfaction of having saved Mr McKay from absolute ruin. He seemed to be on the way to recovery. She wouldn't go as far as to trust him on his own. But so far, so good.

Afterwards, he came through to the kitchen for the cleaning powder to clean out the bath.

'I could have done that, Mr McKay.'

'Certainly not. You do more than enough for me, Miss Eden. It won't take me a minute and it'll be ready for you in the morning.'

They said goodnight but Miss Eden waited until she was sure Mr McKay was safely in bed before she went to her room and settled to sleep.

In the morning, she was always glad when Mr McKay appeared obviously rested and looking a little better and more like himself every day. They had a relaxed breakfast, then cleared the table and did the dishes. She washed and Mr McKay dried. She carefully locked up as they left to cross the road and catch the train to Queen Street.

'You're very convenient for the station, Miss Eden.'

'Yes, and at the Queen Street end as well. It doesn't take long to walk from there to Glassford Street.'

'No, indeed. Very convenient.'

'I'll take some time off in the middle of the day to do some shopping, if that's all right, Mr McKay.'

'Of course. Of course.'

'Mainly for Christmas food. I'd like to get a hamper from Marks & Spencer's. I like their food, don't you?'

'Oh indeed I do.'

'Right. I take it you'll enjoy the usual turkey and all the trimmings and Christmas pudding and brandy butter?'

'You must let me pay for all that, Miss Eden. I insist.'

'You insisted on paying far too much for your board and lodging, Mr McKay. It's perfectly sufficient to cover the Christmas dinner.'

'But really, Miss Eden, I do feel I'm imposing on your generosity.'

'Nonsense. I'll be having the meal anyway and it'll be much more enjoyable to share it.'

'Well, if you're sure.'

'Perfectly sure.'

'Well, please take as much time off as you wish.'

'I'll report off and on as usual so that you know when I'm on duty. It's always worse at this time of year. Shoplifters will be on duty all right, but don't worry. I always catch them.'

'I know, Miss Eden. You are an excellent detective.'

'Thank you, Mr McKay.'

There was definite satisfaction in both their voices.

28

The Merchant City area of Glasgow had to be where Abi would consider buying a flat. For one thing, it was in the Merchant City that the store was situated. It was also, in her opinion, the most interesting and historic area. There was the Cathedral, from where Bishop Beaton fled to Paris at the time of the Reformation. From the Cathedral, he rescued a number of sacred articles. They included pieces of the Cross of Christ, a casket containing some of the Virgin Mary's hair, part of the girdle of the Virgin, and a fragment of St Bartholomew's skin. There was also a bone of St Magdalene, milk from the Virgin, part of the manger in which Jesus was born, and fluid which seeped from the tomb of St Mungo.

In front of the Cathedral was where they used to burn witches and heretics. Glasgow's Witch Finder was the Reverend Cooper. He had been so efficient at catching witches and making them confess that he became known as 'Burning Cooper'.

It was enough to put anyone off religion, Abi thought, and she recalled the words of Robert Burns, 'Man's inhumanity to man makes countless thousands mourn!'

At the back of the Cathedral was the Necropolis (City of the Dead). It had originally been an old pleasure ground and the cemetery was designed to be a place of peace and inspiration for the local citizens.

Across the road was the ancient house called Provand's Lordship. Mary, Queen of Scots had stayed there, and it was believed that while she was in Provand's Lordship she wrote the 'Casket Letters' which were supposed to reveal that she was having an affair with Lord Bothwell. It was also claimed that the letters implicated her in the murder of her husband, Lord Darnley.

Just beyond Albion Street was the University of Strathclyde's Ramshorn Theatre. Under the pavement outside the Ramshorn Graveyard were the graves of the Foulis brothers, printers to the University and founders of a school of art and design. On one side of the Cathedral was the huge Royal Infirmary. On the other side was the award-winning St Mungo Museum of Religious Life and Art. It aimed to promote respect between people of different faiths or none.

Among the many fascinating places in the area was the Trades House. Then there were the City Halls lining one side of the street called Candleriggs. Many celebrities had appeared in the City Halls, including Charles Dickens, Niccolo Paganini, Oscar Wilde and Harriet Beecher Stowe, who wrote *Uncle Tom's Cabin* and who came to gain support in Glasgow for her campaign against slavery.

Abi had no doubt whatsoever that if she was going to move, it would have to be to the Merchant City area. It was just bringing herself to actually make the move. That was the problem. She wondered how Mr Webster was getting on with his move. He had no choice, of course. He and his family would not be able to afford living in an expensive hotel indefinitely.

She felt tempted to call at the hotel to see him, mention to him that she was thinking of moving herself, and even ask for his advice. There were various new developments in the area.

There was also the Italian Centre with designer shops and a restaurant surrounding an interior courtyard with flats looking down on to it. The restaurant had tables outside too, with canopies protecting them from sun or rain. The outside eating arrangements weren't used much in the winter, though. But it was altogether an attractive centre. She understood that the flats were popular with business people who came to Glasgow on business trips, but eventually would have to move on to a base in another city. So there was usually a chance of buying a flat there. And of course, with entrances on Ingram Street, it was very convenient for Glassford Street and the Goodmans store.

Several times, she hovered around the Italian Centre, pretending to study what was in the shop windows. Once she actually went through into the courtyard and gazed up at all the flat windows. Another time, she had a cup of coffee in one of the restaurants. Then she returned to the store and her office, did some paperwork, and made a few business phone calls.

Later, at home, she switched on all the lights, shut all the curtains, and then switched on the television. It drowned out the sound of the wind, and the trees tapping monotonously on the windows.

She made a cup of tea and sat drinking it, and writing in her notebook.

Vote, vote, vote for Harry Lauder,
Vote, vote, vote for all his men.
Then we'll buy a penny gum,
And we'll shoot him up the bum,
And we'll never see old Harry any more.

She looked at 'The Jeely Piece Song' again and penned the second verse.

On the first day Maw flung oot a daud o' Hovis broon,
It cam skitin' oot the windae an' went up instead o' doon.
Now every twenty-seven 'oors it comes back intae sight,
'Cause ma piece went intae orbit an' became a satellite.

Then a repeat of the chorus:

Oh ye cannae fling pieces oot a twenty storey flat,
Seven hundred hungry weans'll testify tae that.
If it's butter, cheese or jeely, if the breid is plain or pan,
The odds against it reachin' earth are ninety-nine tae wan.

'The Jeely Piece Song' always made her smile. She could remember the time in the old tenements when children would shout up to their mothers to throw them down something to eat because they were hungry. The mothers would spread a slice, or a couple of slices of bread with butter or margarine and jam, or jeely to use the Scottish word. Then they'd wrap the sandwich or 'piece' in newspaper and toss it from the kitchen window.

Abi could just imagine how this would be impossible in the high-rise or tower blocks of flats. Not everyone would remember life in the old tenements, though. The song was written in such broad Scots too, she doubted if many people would understand it.

John had said there could be a glossary at the back of the book giving a translation of any difficult Scots words. Or the translation could be in a margin at the right-hand side of each page.

She started another, smaller, notebook with the translation of some words.

Maw	mother
cam	came
daud	lump

oot	out
skitin'	darting through the air suddenly
windae	window
'oors	hours
weans	children
breid	bread

She could still hear the trees thumping and scraping against the windows. Suddenly she could see herself, as if she was outside herself, looking down on herself and the scene inside the room. It was such a picture of pathetic isolation, she suddenly burst into tears.

The proposed book was nonsense. The television was blaring out football, something she was not in the slightest bit interested in. She moaned to herself. There was nothing to compel her attention and engage her feelings. Except her Horatio, who so compellingly, so sympathetically brought Tom back to her. She stumbled over to the television and soon he was there, just like Tom, tall and slim, tenderness, compassion, and understanding radiating from every muscle, every bone of his body.

'Oh, Tom.'

She touched the television screen but it was cold and unresponsive. And she knew she could not go on like this and she would have to start the process of moving.

She decided to get started the first thing next morning. She would not ask Douglas Benson for help or advice. He would try to persuade her to buy a house that was miles away from the store. She could just hear him. 'It would be so good for your health to live your remaining years by the seaside. Good bracing fresh air.' Or 'A little country cottage would be perfect for you. All that peace and quiet. It would do you the world of good.'

Do him the world of good, he'd mean. Yet she felt so unlike

her normal energetic, capable, efficient self. She needed help and advice. Next day, instead of going across the square towards Ingram Street and Glassford Street, she forced her feet into the Millennium Hotel.

Mr Webster strode towards her, his handsome features showing both surprise and concern.

'Don't worry, Mr Webster,' she said. 'I'm not here to sack you or anything like that. Quite the reverse. I need your help and advice.'

'Anything I can do, Mrs Goodman . . . I'm more than willing to do anything I possibly can to help you. But first of all, can I get you a cup of tea?'

'Thank you, Mr Webster.'

He led her by the arm across to one of the chairs and gently sat her down before going to give an order to the waiter at the serving counter. He had no sooner settled himself in a chair opposite Abi when the waiter appeared at the table with a tray that held a pot of tea, cups and saucers, and milk and sugar. He set everything out in front of them, poured the tea, and then left, carrying the empty tray.

Mr Webster said, 'Now, Mrs Goodman, tell me how I can help you.'

'Well . . .' She hesitated. 'I've been feeling somewhat unhappy and isolated in the house in Huntershill since my husband's death. I've come to the conclusion that I should move to a more central location, and perhaps a smaller house. I thought perhaps a flat somewhere in the Merchant City.'

'That sounds a sensible idea. Somewhere nearer to the store, are you thinking of?'

'Yes. That would be ideal.'

'Don't worry. I'll help you all I can. There is a new, very modern conversion I could show you. Then there's the Italian Centre and the flats in the square. To mention just a few locations.'

'I like the situation of the Italian Centre. Have you seen inside any of the flats there?'

'As a matter of fact, I have. There's a luxury one going at the moment. The entry date is a bit further on but if you're not wanting to move immediately . . . The flat is a bit out of my league in my present circumstances. I'm looking at flats in the High Street at the moment. There are older properties that need a bit of work but that's reflected in the asking price, which suits me better.'

'I'd like to view the one in the Italian Centre.'

'I'll arrange that for you right away, and I'll go with you.'

'Thank you, Mr Webster.'

'It's the least I can do after you were so kind and helpful to me.'

'I don't want to involve my family.'

'I quite understand. I'll see to all the arrangements. You won't need to worry about anything. I'll come out to Huntershill and see what needs to be done there. Perhaps you won't have room for all your furniture if you get the flat in the Italian Centre. That would mean you'd have to choose what you're going to keep, and so on. Or there's the option of starting afresh and buying all new furniture and furnishings for the flat. But one step at a time. We must see about getting you the flat first. It's a popular place and flats there are usually snapped up immediately.'

He dug a mobile phone from an inside pocket.

'I'll get on to it right now.'

Abi felt a flutter of panic.

29

'I would have asked John,' Abi said, 'but he is inundated with work and there's been all the upset and worry about the murder as well.'

They had been to see the flat and Mr Webster had contacted his solicitor and instructed him to put in an offer on her behalf. She had not wanted to use the Goodman family solicitor in case Douglas Benson got to know about it.

The offer was accepted.

'Have they found anybody for the murder yet?' Mr Webster asked eventually. 'I believe there's a reward been offered.'

'Not as far as I know.'

Her mind was not really on the conversation. Everything was happening too quickly. All right, she had been thinking about moving, swithering about it for what seemed ages. But suddenly it was actually happening and she didn't feel ready. Not really. Not in her mind. How could she give up Tom's house? The house his father had built and that had always been part of the family's history and background. She kept fingering the engagement ring Tom had given her. It had a huge cluster of diamonds in a setting which needed mending. It had become sharp and jaggy. But she couldn't even bear to take it off and give it to a jeweller to fix.

Mr Webster didn't understand. He was so enthusiastic, so

obviously eager to repay her for what she'd done for him. She had done nothing really, except perhaps save him from Douglas Benson. She knew, and he knew, that Douglas Benson would have sacked him.

But he didn't understand that while it was one thing accepting the fact that moving from Huntershill was the sensible thing to do in her circumstances, it was quite another making it a reality, making it actually happen. And so quickly.

She felt confused. Why on earth had she spoken to Mr Webster? She'd seen the day when she never had any doubts about anything. She knew what she wanted and went after it, made snap decisions, never asked anyone's advice or opinion. Never cared. Had a hundred per cent confidence in herself.

She felt frightened at getting old. She felt she was becoming a completely different person. If anyone had told her ten years ago that she would become like this, she would not have believed them. 'No way,' she would have scoffed. 'Not me.'

Of course, the shock of Tom dying and the terrible feeling of loss had contributed to how she was now. To be without Tom had changed her life. It was impossible to be the same without him. Then Douglas Benson's hardening attitude towards her and his determination to ruin everything that Tom and his father before him had built up had obviously had an effect on her.

Benson would be furious at her moving so near to the store. It would have made him happy if she had retired and moved to the Bahamas or Australia, anywhere as far from the store as possible. He wanted rid of her.

'You'll know such a difference,' Mr Webster was saying. 'I know Huntershill and the house you're in just now. I've passed up that way a couple of times in the car on my way to do a bit of business in Bishopbriggs. The house can't have any outlook, surrounded by all those high bushes and trees. You'll find it so much cheerier and more interesting looking out the windows of the flat.'

It was all perfectly true and sensible. Yet she still couldn't believe it was going to happen. The person who was selling the flat had been offered a job abroad, apparently. He was starting in a month or two. It was as if everything was conspiring against her. Or was it for her? She didn't know. She wasn't sure of anything any more. Except that she was frightened.

Christmas had come and gone and she hardly remembered what she had done. Douglas Benson and Minna had taken the children to London to spend Christmas with Douglas's brother. She hadn't told John this so that he wouldn't feel guilty about not spending it with her. He had been invited to various parties in his constituency. She knew he would have cancelled everything to be with her. He had asked her if she'd be spending Christmas with the children and she'd said yes because at the time she had taken it for granted that she would be.

John had added, 'Now, are you sure, Mum, because I don't want you to be on your own? I'll cancel everything and come through to be with you in Huntershill. Or you can come to Edinburgh – whichever you prefer. Just let me know.'

The news was sprung on her – almost at the last moment – that Benson and his family were not having her at Christmas but were going away to London. She didn't feel then that it would be fair to John to spoil his Christmas and so she didn't tell him about the last-minute change of plans.

As a result, she had the worst Christmas of her life. It had been an absolute agony of grief and loneliness. She didn't know what she would have done without her dear, kind Horatio for company. She supposed, in a way, that the awful Christmas, the desperation she'd suffered, had been what forced her to make her final decision.

'Now, when do you want me to come out to Huntershill?'

Mr Webster was saying now. She was back in the hotel for yet another meeting. They could meet in private there without arousing any curiosity, any suspicion from Douglas Benson, or anyone else in the store. She needed to get everything done and dusted (to use Mr Webster's words) to avoid any difficulties being put in her way, or any distress being caused to her by Benson. She was really very grateful to Mr Webster. She had always known that he was an excellent and conscientious employee. Now she was finding him a good, kind friend.

She was able, as a result, to testify to his good and trustworthy character in the court case against the South Castle-on-Sea woman who had been tormenting him. The woman had escaped a jail sentence, helped perhaps by her tearful apologies and pleas for mercy. She had been given community service and served with a restraining order preventing her going near Mr Webster again.

He hadn't been down in South Castle-on-Sea since and she hoped the woman had learned her lesson by now. Needless to say, Mr Webster was hoping the same thing.

'Let's hope, Mr Webster,' Abi tried to sound positive, 'that her stay in a police cell and the threat of a jail sentence if she comes near you again will make her see sense.'

He made the effort but failed to appear a hundred per cent confident. 'Yes, and there's her business to consider. She can't continue neglecting that or she'll go broke.'

'And now people are starting to think about summer holidays, she's bound to be getting bookings.'

'Yes, people have to book early these days, especially in South Castle-on-Sea. It's a very popular place for holidays.'

'So just put the whole business out of your head and stop worrying.'

She was a fine one to talk. She worried continuously.

At least Mr Webster was happily settled in a flat. After a bit of haggling, his offer had been accepted and he had bought furniture and all the household goods and some clothes that he and the family urgently needed, all at very reduced prices from Goodmans. She had insisted on that, despite Benson's bitter comments that if she went on as she was doing, she would end up being the ruination of the store. He always added, 'It's high time you gave up and retired.'

Mr Webster's daughters were back at university and Mrs Webster had a part-time job in Books and Stationery.

'Just until you get back on your feet,' Abi had told her when Mrs Webster had protested.

'You've done too much for us already, Mrs Goodman. I don't want to take advantage.'

'You're not taking advantage. We need an extra hand in Books and Stationery just now. At least for a couple of afternoons a week. Somebody to tidy and replenish the bookshelves and the stationery counter. You'll earn your pay.'

'When do you want me to come over to help clear the Huntershill house?' Mr Webster repeated. 'You obviously can't take everything with you to your new place.'

'Well . . .' She didn't want to say because, ridiculous though it sounded, she still didn't believe it was happening. Leaving Tom's home and all the memories it held. No, surely not.

'How about right now? You weren't planning on going back to the shop again today, were you? There's no urgent business you've to attend to that can't be put off until tomorrow, is there?'

'Well, no . . .'

'Right then. My car's parked round the corner. Let's go.'

Abi could have wept. She knew it was totally unfair, but just at the moment, she hated Mr Webster. She was silent all during the drive to Huntershill. She was conscious of Mr Webster glancing round at her several times. But she did not respond and he made no attempt to force conversation.

Once at the house, however, he couldn't contain himself.

'Mrs Goodman, I don't know how you've managed to stick it out here for so long on your own. It's really spooky.'

She unlocked the door and he followed her inside. Once in the drawing room, he said, 'This is a lovely room, right enough. All that artistic cornicing. But you're lucky. The Italian Centre flats are listed and they have the same features. Is that a picture of your late husband's father?'

'Yes. Tom Senior who founded Goodmans.'

'A fine looking gentleman.'

'Yes, he was.'

And so was my Tom, she thought. Tall and slim, with a quirky smile that was reflected in his eyes. He had a way of leaning forward and listening with genuine and sympathetic interest to whoever was speaking to him – even if it was the most junior employee. It didn't matter if it was a manager or a cleaner. He had that same gentle concentration. Just like Horatio.

'I wonder if that settee and those easy chairs will fit into the sitting room in the flat?' Mr Webster was walking around staring at everything. 'They're very attractive and comfortable-looking. But extremely large, aren't they? Have you got a measuring tape anywhere, Mrs Goodman?'

'Yes, I've one in the sewing box over there beside that chair.'

Mr Webster went over to where she had indicated. After retrieving the tape, he began taking measurements of the chairs and other pieces of furniture and writing everything down in his notebook.

He did the same in the other rooms, including the five bedrooms. She left her own bedroom till last. She felt it a terrible intrusion to show anyone into such a private place. It had been the room where she had shared so many loving and passionate nights with Tom.

'Of course, with only three bedrooms in the flat, you'll have to get rid of a couple of the bedroom suites you have here. I'd keep the brass beds. They've become fashionable again. But forgive me, Mrs Goodman. There's a dreadful amount of clutter that you'll have to get rid of. I know it's all very attractive and no doubt worth a lot of money . . .'

Oh, more than money, she thought. Oh, so much more.

'And I've no doubt much of it is also of great sentimental value, but it's a matter of the space available in your flat compared to here. This is a very big house.'

'Yes, I quite understand,' she agreed politely. But she didn't understand at all. It was a nightmare scenario. She wanted it to stop. Not happen. Cancel everything. But there were already people booked to view the house. She dreaded doing the viewings but Mr Webster had promised to be with her.

The first people who came were a young couple who said they were into selling. Something to do with the internet. Abi couldn't make head nor tail of what they were talking about. No doubt Benson would have known. He knew all about the internet and God knew all what else that could be done with computers. She hated the things and, if anything needed to be typed, she had her secretary do it.

For anything that wasn't related to business, like personal letters and, of course, the silly book of poems and songs, she wrote longhand. Though she'd probably have to get the poems and songs typed up before sending them off to a publisher. John said that email was used for that nowadays. He was certainly nagging her about the project, as he called it. Every time he saw her, he asked her how she was getting on with it.

It had been an agony showing the couple round the house. They were obviously going to change the whole atmosphere of the place. They said things to each other like, 'This room could be your office. And this one could be mine . . .'

It wasn't going to be like a home at all.

Abi felt quite ill after the experience and told Mr Webster she didn't want to show anyone else around. He said not to worry, there was no need. He would see to that side of it, and the solicitor would no doubt advise her to accept the highest offer.

And so it was done. There was no turning back. The house was sold.

30

Robert Louis Stevenson had once said, 'There are no stars so lovely as Edinburgh street lamps.' Right enough, Edinburgh was a lovely city. Abi had stayed with John the night before and had seen for herself how beautiful the city could be at night, as well as during the day. A bit frightening too, in the Old Town at least, with its dark, narrow alleyways and half-hidden closes or wynds. John had taken her out for dinner, but had previously warned her not to wander about on her own after dark. The police still hadn't caught Julie's killer and had come to the conclusion that they had a serial killer on their hands. Three women had now been killed around the Royal Mile area.

'There might be more hope of finding him now with their knowledge of DNA,' John had said. 'They even took a sample from me.'

'For goodness' sake!' Abi shook her head. 'I thought they'd realised by now that you had nothing whatever to do with poor Julie's death.'

She had come through to Edinburgh on Mr Webster's advice. The removers were coming first thing in the morning and he said it would be better if she wasn't there when they came. It might be a little upsetting for her.

A little? She couldn't even bear to think about it. By now, it would have happened. By the time she returned to Glasgow, it would have to be to the flat in the Italian Centre. It had been bad enough picking out what to keep and what to discard or sell or abandon among the furniture and furnishings and personal belongings. Mr Webster advised her to stay in Edinburgh for another couple of nights to give him time to have the carpets laid and the curtains hung and so on. The only areas to be carpeted, though, were the bedrooms. The rest of the flat had shiny parquet flooring with only a few rugs dotted here and there.

John had agreed that, although it was a wrench, even for him, to see the old house go, it was the most sensible thing to do. It was best for her sake. She had definitely been getting depressed and he had been worried about her.

'It's very good that you've had Mr Webster helping so much. He's very efficient, isn't he?'

'Yes. I couldn't have done it without him. I didn't dare tell Douglas Benson. He would have created such a fuss about me moving nearer to the store.'

'I'm sorry that I couldn't be more help, Mum. I feel guilty about that.'

'No, no. There's no need to feel guilty, son. You haven't as much time as Mr Webster and you've done what you could. I employ Mr Webster to help me.'

John smiled. 'Moving house for you is not supposed to be on his list of duties though, Mum.'

'I know, but he offered and said I'd helped him more than I needed to. He lost his home . . .'

'God, I know. I read about it. That woman must be really crazy. Has he got anywhere else yet?'

'Yes, quite a nice red sandstone flat in the High Street. He took me to see it. His wife gave me afternoon tea. A very nice woman.'

A strong and courageous woman, she thought. After all, not only had her husband been unfaithful to her but she had also lost her home. She had lost everything she'd built up over the years.

Abi wished she had not promised Mr Webster that she would stay an extra couple of nights in Edinburgh. John would be late getting home tonight because he had a previous engagement he couldn't get out of. She didn't like being in his flat on her own. She had assured him that she would be perfectly all right, of course, and she didn't mind a bit. What a liar she had become.

It was all right during the day. She enjoyed a walk around the city admiring the views. Edinburgh was like Rome in one way. It was built on seven hills. Three of these hills reared up in the centre of the city – Castle Rock, Arthur's Seat and Calton Hill. The other four – Corstorphine Hill (where the zoo was situated), Blackford Hill (site of the Royal Observatory), Braid Hill and Wester Craiglockhart – were only a few minutes by bus run from the centre.

The highest hill was Arthur's Seat. It was, like Calton Hill, an ancient volcanic plug. From any of these hills, the views were interesting and picturesque. Each part of the city was linked to the next by hundreds of steps and spectacular bridges.

At different times, John had taken her for walks around the city. He'd also shown her fascinating views from places like the Outlook Tower and the Camera Obscura. No wonder so many tourists flooded into Edinburgh every year. Not only tourists, of course. Many English people and people from other countries had come to study here, or work in the medical, legal and other professions.

The time John liked best was during the Festival and he got tickets for the Military Tattoo at the Castle every year. Abi enjoyed the spectacle, which was rich in colour, tradition, music and excitement under the floodlights of the Castle Esplanade.

John also took her to various Fringe events. He was very fond of jazz, but she could not share his pleasure and excitement in that. The energy of the music seemed to tune in perfectly to his own enthusiastic and energetic nature. It hadn't been Tom's favourite kind of music either. She supposed Tom was more 'cool' and 'laid back', to use a couple of popular expressions she'd heard. Yes, he was cool and laid back. Like Horatio.

Thinking of Tom made her remember her home at Huntershill again. Her heart immediately contracted with pain. It wasn't her home any more. She struggled to return her thoughts and attention to her immediate surroundings.

The day had become wet and windy and, although it wasn't late, the sky was darkening. Abi shivered. It always seemed colder in Edinburgh. Probably it was just because of the east wind.

The tall, ancient buildings rising up all around her suddenly had a claustrophobic effect. Not only did the buildings crowd in on her, but their history too. She felt all the characters of ancient and often barbaric times come to life and hustle for attention. Each one had a story to tell – from the poorest servants and soldiers, to the highest clergy and royalty in the land.

She had been viewing the buildings and reading about them and their history too much. She had been speaking with John about them too much. Or rather, John had been speaking to her about them too much. He certainly knew his Scotland and particularly its capital very well indeed. It was all a part of his ardent Scottish Nationalism.

She admired how he could convey his enthusiasm in the chamber, and even come out with the most provocative, to some even outrageous, statements – without losing his temper. He was obviously able to keep himself strictly under control and suppress any anger while he was in the debating chamber. But oh, he could never suppress or contain his enthusiasm.

She remembered him as a little boy when Santa brought him a gift that he had longed for. Oh, the way he had danced up and down! The way he had screeched with delight and clapped his hands, his happiness spilling over as he hugged everyone and showered them with kisses.

Minna, who was older than John, used to cringe with embarrassment. Minna's quiet common sense had not saved her, however, from marrying a selfish bully who wouldn't even allow her to have a normal social life with her own mother. She looked anything but happy. John, on the other hand, had always looked very happy indeed. He had been sad at what happened to his secretary, of course, and worried too about the attitude of the police. But he was even getting over that and he had another secretary now.

'She isn't Julie, Mum. No one could replace her. She was so conscientious and never complained about the long hours she often had to work. But this girl will be fine, I'm sure. Once she gets a bit more experience.'

It was definitely getting dark. Abi thought it was time she returned to John's flat. To get there from where she now found herself meant going through a couple of narrow closes and wynds. Suddenly she felt nervous. She had been wandering about for too long and not paying attention to where she was going or the amount of time that was passing. In one of the wynds, she was startled by a group of hunkered figures furtively drinking in the shadows. She quickened her pace. Then, getting out of breath, she stood at the top of the steps, the wind funnelling through the arch behind her. She heard slow steps and – frighteningly – rasping, heavy breathing. She tensed nervously; what to do – fight or flight? Before she could rationalise further, a bunneted shape materialised.

'Jeez, hen, these steps fair bring on yer asthma.'

She laughed with relief. The man had a Glasgow accent. He was probably, like her, in Edinburgh for the day and having a look around Edinburgh's historic streets and wynds.

'Aye,' she answered in an equally Glaswegian accent. 'Ye're right there.'

What a foolish woman she was, she thought, as she walked on. After all John's concern, here she was doing exactly what he had warned her not to do. Wandering about in the dark.

Even knowing about Julie's murder and the other murders in this very area, here she was, having allowed her mind as well as her feet to wander dangerously. It wasn't even as it if was a story. The murders were real. They had really happened.

She began to run and by the time she reached John's close and hastily climbed his stairs, she was gasping for breath and sweat was dripping over her eyes. She fumbled desperately to put her key in the lock. At last, thankfully, she was inside. She leaned her back against the door with relief.

It took her quite a few minutes to get her breath back, before she was able to go into the kitchen. There, instead of making a cup of tea, she poured herself a stiff whisky. It brought soothing warmth and comfort. It calmed her down. She didn't feel any happier, however. It worried her so much how she had changed. She had always been a calm, courageous woman. Everyone said so. She certainly never used to be a worrier.

She switched on the light in the small sitting room and collapsed into a chair. She ought to have returned to Glasgow and faced the house move. Now she worried about Mr Webster's supervision of all her belongings. Her *CSI: Miami* DVDs for instance. She was very fond of them. They were like old friends. Horatio was definitely a much-loved old friend.

She rummaged in her handbag. Earlier in the day she had come across a healthfood and vitamin store and had bought a herbal sedative. She went through to the kitchen and swallowed a couple of the tablets down with a glass of water.

She already had sleeping tablets from the doctor but she had left them in the bathroom cabinet in Huntershill. Had Mr Webster remembered to pack the medical cabinet and its contents? She closed her eyes and took another tablet.

31

It wasn't always the shoplifters coming into the shop that Miss Eden had to keep her eye on. It could be workmen doing a job. It could be staff. Staff were most difficult to stop. Fortunately, it was only on a few occasions that a member of staff let the side down. She had in fact to depend on staff tipping her off if they had suspicions about somebody. Once told of a suspicion, however, it was up to her to observe the person. She couldn't take her eyes off them for a second. If she saw someone stealing, however, she couldn't stop them until they were outside the store. The problem was that the thief could go to another department where there was a changing room and get rid of the goods. So she had to stick with them. If she wasn't a hundred per cent sure, she couldn't stop anyone. Ninety per cent was not good enough.

Then there was the needle thing. She had to be careful of that all the time inside the shop. They were carried by people who had a drug problem and had to steal to raise more money to feed their habit. Usually staff members didn't fight or threaten her, but pleaded for her to turn a blind eye.

'Please, oh please, Miss Eden, don't report me and make me lose my job.'

'You've committed a crime,' she'd tell them. 'It's up to you to bear the consequences. I'm only doing my job.'

There were times with other people when she really could not understand why they did it. She had read about film stars pinching things in the shops on the famous Rodeo Drive. It used to be said about women, when they got to the menopause, their hormones were all mixed up and they went off their heads. It was believed that it was an attention-seeking thing. Miss Eden could honestly say she had never come across that.

Apart from the desperate need some people had to feed a drug habit, the motivation was usually just greed. The thieves she had known over the years made more money than she did and she worked hard every day. They could come in and lift something in one day worth more than she earned each month. She knew them, all right, and they knew her. The men would come into the store, see her, and say with good humour, 'Well, I'm wasting my time here.'

In fact, strange though it seemed, once they got to know her in court, she became their bosom buddy and they treated her with respect. Women were not really so good-tempered. The old, down-and-out, homeless women were glad to be nicked and given a bed for the night in the police cells. They were pathetically grateful. It was the other women, some well off, who could be difficult, often nasty, and even dangerous.

Then there were young children of both sexes. They reminded her of Oliver Twist and the Artful Dodger in the novel by Charles Dickens. The sad thing and the problem was that their parents didn't care about them and they would grow up knowing nothing else, no other way of life. They would form into gangs and end up as gangsters. They would spend much of their lives in prison. Whereas, if they had been taken into decent homes and given a chance . . .

She had to be careful that the children didn't get into the lift and end up in the staff area. There, despite repeated warnings and reminders, one member of staff or another would leave their key in their locker. As a result, they would find by evening that their purses and wallets had disappeared.

There was a warning system in Glassford Street and Argyle Street. If a known shoplifter was seen in Marks & Spencer's, for instance, and they didn't manage to get anything there, the security guard or detective would watch them going along the road. If they saw them going into Goodmans, they would phone and warn her.

This continuous alertness could be very exhausting, even before the arrest of any culprit. Miss Eden was glad to get home and relax. With Mr McKay to watch as well, it had been an extra strain. He had been her lodger for quite a time and, apart from a few setbacks at first, he was really fine now. On one occasion in the early days, he'd tried to sneak a bottle of Buckfast into her house. She'd found it and, before his eyes, she'd poured it down the kitchen sink.

'We'll be civilised, Mr McKay. We'll have a glass of wine with our evening meal. All right?'

He had looked embarrassed and ashamed. 'Yes, of course, Miss Eden.'

After that, they had enjoyed the evening glass of wine. She bought small bottles, just enough for one glass each. They even had interesting discussions about what wine to purchase, sometimes red, sometimes white. Sometimes Italian, some-times Australian. A Merlot was one of their favourites.

They'd got into the habit of going to the karate club two or three times a week, and she suspected that Mr McKay actually enjoyed these visits. She remembered the first occasion. She had pushed through the swing doors into the community centre.

'How're you today, Archie?' she'd ask the familiar figure sitting behind the counter.

'No' bad, hen. No' bad. Ye're late the day; ye're aye first here.'

Archie, the facilities officer, or in old-speak the janitor, had his hands clasped over his little round belly, cheery face, a mesh of broken veins across his nose. Only his grey brush-cut hair spoiled the likeness to a rather debauched Santa.

'Yes, but I've a friend with me today. He's only going to watch. This is Mr McKay. Mr McKay, I'm going to get into my gi. If you go through to the left, there's a wee café where you can get a cup of tea or whatever.'

As she strode confidently into the Ladies, he entered the café.

On the right-hand wall were several large, narrow windows that allowed a view of the sports hall. Mr McKay told Miss Eden later that he had drawn up a stool and leant forward to get a better view. He was interested to see that there was a children's class just finishing, with rows of mini white-pyjamaed figures stamping up and down with intense expressions. He was impressed, he said, by the effort and commitment of the youngsters. In spite of himself, he admitted he felt a growing curiosity to see what the senior class might accomplish.

As time went on, Miss Eden toyed with the idea of suggesting to Mr McKay that he should join the beginners' class. It could be something else for him to concentrate on. It would also increase his self-confidence and his self-worth.

It had to be said, though, that he was more or less back to normal. She had begun to wonder if he had settled in too happily to life as her lodger. After a few months, she had encouraged him to pay his own home a visit – just to see how he'd feel. She'd gone with him, even followed him as he wandered about each room. He had looked somewhat distressed the first time, and was obviously glad to get back to her place in Springburn. The next time, he had looked sad but altogether calmer. He insisted, however, that he still did not feel ready to return to the house and live there.

He had begun to talk about his wife too, first about her distressing illness and eventually about their happier times. He told Miss Eden what a brave, positive, happy character his wife had. Miss Eden had encouraged him to be the same, reminding him that his wife would want him to be strong and positive and happy. More recently he had stopped talking about his wife, except perhaps to make the occasional fond but perfectly calm remark about some trivial thing like, 'Jenny used to really enjoy that brand of chocolate.'

Sometimes he even laughed at some eccentric taste she had had. But mostly he was just getting on with his life now. In the evening, over their meal, they usually discussed the day's events at the store.

They had shaken heads and tutted at the scandal concerning Mr Webster and voiced sympathy for his wife. They shared surprise at Mrs Goodman's uncharacteristic attitude to the event and the adverse publicity it caused. Nowadays, in fact, Mrs Goodman seemed to be quite friendly with Mr Webster. Douglas Benson didn't like the situation at all and was very suspicious about it. This was proved by the sly questions he had aimed at Mr McKay. Mr McKay had been no help to him about what Mrs Goodman was up to – not because he was purposely being unhelpful – he just didn't know the answer. Mrs Goodman hadn't been herself for a while. She had taken quite a lot of time off and it was certainly unusual for her to have a personal friendship with a member of staff. But as far as Mr McKay could see, she was now quite attentive and efficient when she was in the store.

'I heard that Mr Webster is now living in the High Street,' Miss Eden said.

'Yes, that's right,' Mr McKay agreed. 'He reported his change of address for the records. Terrible business that, losing his lovely home in Bearsden.'

'And everything he owned. Except his car.'

'He'll know a difference in a flat. There's not a garden for a start, and there'll be less room.'

'Oh, I don't know,' Miss Eden said. 'Those old flats can be pretty roomy. Bigger rooms than in modern houses, and with high ceilings and lovely cornicing.'

'True enough.'

'I don't know how Mrs Goodman managed in that huge isolated place in Huntershill. Have you seen it, Mr McKay?'

'No, I haven't.'

'I once visited a friend who lived at the end of that road and she called for me in her car and drove me home afterwards. We passed it twice – once in the dark.' She shuddered. 'I just caught a glimpse of it through the trees. It looked quite ghastly.'

'Oh dear. At least my house wasn't as bad as that.'

She noticed his use of the past tense.

'And of course,' Mr McKay said, 'a garden is a lot of work. By the way, I phoned about a gardener. He came to the store this morning and we arranged about payment and so on. I just want the grass cut and the place kept tidy. He's got a van, apparently, and can take his own equipment. Though, as I told him, there's a shed at the back where I kept my lawnmower and garden tools.'

The past tense again.

In one way, she wanted to ask him when he was thinking of returning to live in Bishopbriggs. In another way, although she had always been quite happy living on her own, it was quite enjoyable having company.

As well as that, of course, she didn't want to hurry him before he was fit and ready to face life on his own. He had done so well up until now. She didn't want to risk undoing all her (and his) good work.

They had got into such a pleasant routine. Every evening, she put the kettle on. He began setting the table. She got the food started – usually something from Marks & Spencer's that she could pop into the microwave. She bought the pudding from M & S as well. They both enjoyed the food from there, and of course the shop was so handy. It was easy to walk the short distance down Glassford Street to the side entrance of M & S.

While Mr McKay cleared the dirty dishes from the table, she made the tea or coffee – whatever they'd decided to have. After their tea or coffee, she washed the dishes and Mr McKay dried them and put them away in the cupboard.

Then, if they weren't going out to the karate club, they would have a chat again about the day's events. They'd watch the television for a time. Eventually, when it was nearly time to retire to their separate rooms, she made a warm, milky drink for them both and they chose a biscuit each from the biscuit tin.

Last thing in the evening, they would go out into the hall together. She would switch off the kitchen light behind her. Mr McKay would turn at his bedroom door and say, 'Goodnight, Miss Eden. Sleep well.'

'Goodnight, Mr McKay. See you in the morning.'

It was quite a pleasant routine and there was really no hurry.

32

Abi had over an hour to spare before lunching with John in the Parliament. She passed the time walking along the Royal Mile and peering down some of the closes. There had been three women murdered in this area but at night, not during the day, when it was one of the busiest streets in the capital. It was the favourite area for tourists. People came from all over the world to explore the Royal Mile.

She was particularly intrigued, as most people were, with Deacon Brodie's Close. He was a great man of his time, highly regarded in the best of Edinburgh society. He was always a welcome guest because he was a very good singer and it was always regretted when the evening came to an end and the host and hostess had to say goodbye to him.

One of Brodie's friends and an eager host had mentioned to Brodie that he was going off that evening to visit the country. Later, however, he was delayed by some business and decided to stay another night in the city. He had been lying awake that night when suddenly, out of the dark silence, he heard a creak, then a jar. Then he detected a faint light. He clambered out of bed and up to a false window which looked into another room. There, by the glimmer of a thief's lantern, he recognised, despite the mask, his good friend, Deacon Brodie.

It was discovered that Brodie was leading a double life. By day, he was a dignified and most respectable member of society. At night, he was leaving the supper tables of his friends the magistrates and others and slinking about the closes by the flicker of a dark lamp, a sly and cunning burglar.

John kept talking about the book about old Scottish ditties, especially from Glasgow, but in her opinion a book on historical characters would be much more interesting. Abi wandered into another cobbled close, trying to think of more stories of characters from Edinburgh's past – anything to prevent her thinking of what was happening in the immediate present in Glasgow.

She could never again go back to the house in Huntershill. When she returned to Glasgow this time, it would be to the flat in the Italian Centre. Mr Webster would be waiting for her there. Everything had been completed. As he said, 'Everything is in its proper place, down to the last dish towel.' Mrs Webster had helped him. 'The woman's touch,' he had said.

Proper place? her thoughts echoed. Her proper place was in Huntershill.

Just then she was suddenly, violently, terrifyingly, jerked back into her present surroundings. Strong hands gripped round her neck. She screamed and hit backwards with one hand, while clutching at the tourniquet round her neck with the other.

A man's voice cried out, 'Shit!'

For a second, he let her go as his hand flew to his eye. She twisted free and ran, still screaming, towards the busy Royal Mile. She just caught a glimpse of the man's face with blood pouring from his eye. Her ring must have jagged into it.

Two men came running towards her, shouting, 'What's happened?'

'That man was trying to kill me.'

But by this time, the man was running off down the close.

The men ran after him and a woman dialled for the police on her mobile phone.

The police arrived within minutes and the woman explained what had happened. Abi had to answer questions and give the police her name and address. By this time, she was seated in a chair, being comforted by another woman. The chair had been brought out from a nearby restaurant and a small crowd of bystanders had formed.

Eventually Abi saw, through the crowd, the police leading a man into their police car. The man was holding a blood-stained handkerchief to his face.

'We'd better phone for an ambulance for you,' one of the women said to Abi.

'No, no. Thank you all the same, but I'm all right now. A cup of tea's all I need. It was just the shock.'

'All right, if you're sure. But me and my friend will come with you into the restaurant. We could do with a cup of tea ourselves. Then we'll see you home.'

The two men who'd caught her attacker arrived on the scene then.

'Are you OK?'

'Yes, thank you so much. That was very brave of you.' She shuddered. 'He must be that man who's been killing women around here.'

'You've been lucky. You might have been the fourth.'

One of the women said, 'You shouldn't have been going down any of the closes on your own while he was on the loose.'

'I know. My mind was full of other things, but who would have thought that anything could happen in broad daylight?'

'Well, there you are, you've had a lucky escape.'

The three of them felt better after a cup of tea, and Abi said, 'Actually, I've to go to the Parliament and meet my son for lunch there. He's an MSP.'

'What's his name?' one of the women asked.

'John Goodman.'

'The Scottish Nationalist?'

'Yes.'

'Gosh, you must be very proud. He's one of the few honest ones in there. He's got courage as well. He's never afraid to speak his mind.'

Abi felt very proud indeed, and very pleased. 'Yes, I am proud. He's always been a good son to me. But he'll be angry at me today. Just because he'll be upset. He worries about me and he's warned me more than once not to wander about the closes on my own. But they're so atmospheric and interesting, aren't they? And as I said, who would have thought that the murderer would be skulking around in broad daylight?'

'Well, you did a good turn in a way, Mrs Goodman. The closes will be safe for everyone to wander about now.'

Abi had taken one of her herbal calming tablets with her tea and felt fine again. Or as fine as she could in the circumstances – the circumstances being what they'd been before. She'd lost the home she'd shared with Tom. It was like losing him again but this time it was really forever. There was nothing at all of Tom in the flat in the Italian Centre.

'We've done our best to help you,' one of the women said. 'Would you mind doing us a favour in return, Mrs Goodman?'

'Of course. If I can.'

'We'd love to meet your son. Wouldn't we, Evie?'

'Oh gosh, yes. We've been admirers of his for ages. We voted for him, didn't we, Mae?'

'Yes, definitely.'

'Of course I'll introduce you. It'll be my pleasure.'

After that, the three of them set off, to all appearances quite happily, down the Royal Mile towards the Parliament.

When they got to the entrance, Abi said, 'What do you think of it? The building, I mean.'

'Oh, very impressive,' Evie said. 'Really different. Out of this world.'

Abi was genuinely surprised at their enthusiasm. Personally she thought it was far too over the top. Except the entrance, which could be so easily walked past and missed from the outside. The entrance, she always thought, should have been much more impressive and noticeable.

John was waiting for her inside and, after giving him his usual hug and kiss, she introduced him to Mae and Evie and explained the circumstances in which they'd met.

John paled visibly. 'Mum, you could have been killed. My God . . .'

'Now, there's no need to worry. I'm perfectly all right and the man has been caught.' She laughed. 'I gave him a punch in the eye and that finished him. I'm always telling you and everyone else that I can cope perfectly well.'

Wait until Douglas Benson hears about this, she thought. She smiled to herself. Not only was she perfectly capable of continuing to run the store, she was even capable of fighting off a murderer, and having him arrested. It would be in the papers. She would be made to appear quite a heroine. It was laughable, of course, but she could hardly wait to see Douglas Benson's face.

In an unexpected way, it would help her to break the news that she had moved to the Italian Centre and would be handier for attending to any business in the store.

After John had recovered from his initial shock and had assured himself that she was none the worse for her experience, he was charming to Mae and Evie and even insisted that they join them for lunch. Mae and Evie were excited and delighted and later, when they parted, they were profuse in their thanks and promises to continue voting for John at every opportunity.

After they'd gone, John said, 'Now, what are you going to

do this afternoon? I don't trust you at all being on your own now.'

'Darling, there's no danger any more. The man's been caught.'

'Yes, but God alone knows what other trouble you could get into.'

She couldn't help laughing.

'Johnny, I'm your mother, not your errant child.'

'My errant mother. What am I going to do with you? You just won't do as you're told.'

'Talking about children reminds me. I wanted to visit the Museum of Childhood. I might be able to get something for the children. Or at least I could describe it all to them. I'm sure it would interest them.'

'Yes, all right. But have you been doing what I told you about compiling a book of verse?'

'Yes, I have.'

'Honestly?'

'Yes, honestly. Next time you're in Glasgow visiting me I'll show it to you. I've actually finished it. You will be coming through soon to visit me at the Italian Centre, I hope?'

'Of course I will, Mum. How about if I go back with you tomorrow?'

'Oh, that would be wonderful, John. I wasn't really looking forward to going into the place for the first time on my own.'

'Well, that's what we'll do and I'll stay overnight if you want me to.'

'Oh, yes please, Johnny.'

'Right, that's what I'll do. We'll definitely travel to Glasgow together tomorrow and I'll stay in your new home – make sure you're happily settled in.'

33

Mr Webster was glad of the opportunity to help Mrs Goodman. In a way, it salved his conscience. It kept him busy and his mind fully occupied. Strangely enough, it brought his wife and him closer together. For the first time in their marriage, they worked together. There had been a great deal to do, first of all in clearing the house. Moira had gone through all the drawers, emptying them and packing the contents into boxes, which she labelled so that they would later know what each box contained. Over innumerable cups of tea, they discussed each find. A whole life was revealed. It was both embarrassing and sad. Mrs Goodman had kept every card her husband had ever sent her or given her on birthdays, anniversary days, Christmas Days, New Year's Days. Or just days when he wanted to tell her how much he loved her. When he had been away on business, he had written love letters to her every day.

Moira said, 'No wonder the poor woman didn't want to face all this. It must have been a terrible blow when he died. They were obviously very much in love right to the end.'

'Yes, you didn't know her then.' Sam said. 'You never met her, did you? Not until all this happened.'

'No.'

'She has changed such a lot. You wouldn't believe how

capable and efficient she was. Quite brusque as well. She didn't suffer fools gladly.'

'What was her husband like?'

'Much the same. Strong and efficient. A hard worker. They were well matched.'

'She must miss him terribly.'

'Yes, and I can imagine how she must be feeling now, giving up the home they shared so happily together.'

'It's an awful spooky place. I mean, with all those trees and high bushes so close to the house.'

'I know. I told her that. It wasn't a happy place for her to be on her own. I think, by the way, that we shouldn't unpack these boxes of cards and letters. We'll keep them in the sealed boxes. To be honest, I'd like to destroy them.'

'Oh, Sam, you couldn't. That would be dreadful.'

He shrugged. 'What's the use of living in the past? It's not doing her any good and it'll never bring him back.'

'I know, but still . . .'

'Anyway, we'll leave them in the sealed boxes and maybe she'll do it herself. Destroy them, I mean. Give up the past and start afresh. That's what she needs to do. Get herself a new life.'

'Not so easy at her age.'

'I'm not sure of her exact age but I think she must be nearing the official retirement age, judging by the way Douglas Benson's going on at her.'

'He doesn't sound like a very nice man.'

'He isn't. But I can understand where he's coming from. Talk about the past! Goodmans is a good example of that.'

'It's a lovely old shop. And customers get immediate and individual attention. Where else do you get that nowadays?'

'Yes, I know, but the profits could be doubled, according to Benson, if he got rid of all the counters and just had pay points. Customers could then search through rails, in the clothes department, for instance, and then take their chosen goods over to the nearest pay point. Think of all the staff he could get rid of and the money he could save that way.'

'Oh, I can see why that idea won't be popular.'

'Yes, I think I'd be all right, being a buyer, but I can appreciate how the rest of the staff feel.'

'And the regular customers. He might lose a lot of customers and not make as much profit as he imagines.'

'Could be. But one wonders how long it will be possible for Mrs Goodman to hold back progress.'

Mrs Webster smiled. 'She might be tougher than we think. She certainly fought back at that Edinburgh murderer, according to the papers. They made her out to be quite a heroine.'

'That must have been a terrible shock to her, all the same. I wonder if she'll stay for a while with her son in Edinburgh. She doesn't seem to be able to keep her mind on the store nowadays. Yet if she did retire, I wonder what she'd do with her life. She doesn't seem to have any friends or even any outside interests. We're talking about her starting a new life but I don't know exactly what kind of new life she could have.'

'Yes, by the looks of things, her life has been completely tied up with her late husband.'

'Oh well, you never know. Living in the flat might make all the difference to her. It's so much cheerier, isn't it? And such an interesting outlook. A great view of life in Ingram Street and Glassford Street on one side, and the courtyard and all those lovely shops and restaurants on the other.'

'We'll see.'

'Are you going to wait until she gets settled in here before going down to South Castle-on-Sea?'

'Yes. I'm not looking forward to going down there again.'

'Would you like me to come with you? A breath of sea

air will do me good, and I've never been to South Castle-on-Sea.'

'Would you, darling? I'd love you to come.'

'That's it settled, then.'

'I'll phone Edinburgh and try to find out when Mrs Goodman is planning to return to Glasgow. She was supposed to get back tomorrow. I told her we'd have everything organised by then, but she may have decided to stay longer with her son.'

As it turned out, Mrs Goodman was returning the next morning and her son was coming with her and staying in the flat with her for a couple of nights, at least.

'That'll solve our problem,' Sam told Moira. 'We won't need to worry about her being on her own until she gets used to the place.'

And so they were able to get ready for the journey to South Castle-on-Sea immediately after welcoming Mrs Goodman and her son into the flat. Sam handed over her keys and said, 'I hope you'll be very happy here, Mrs Goodman.'

'Thank you, Mr Webster. It certainly looks very nice. Thanks for all your hard work.'

'Yes,' John Goodman agreed. 'You've done an excellent job and we both appreciate all your help. And Mrs Webster as well. If ever you fancy a trip to the Parliament, just give me a ring and I'll show you around and give you lunch.'

Mrs Webster smiled. 'We might just do that, Mr Goodman. I've never seen the Parliament except on television. I'd be most interested to pay it a visit.'

'Just give me a ring,' John repeated.

Eventually they got away to drive along to the High Street. Once in their own flat, they had a meal and packed an overnight bag. They left early the next morning and it was still light when they arrived in South Castle-on-Sea.

Sam had already booked them into a hotel he'd stayed in

before. He would have been quite content to sit in the conservatory and look out at the sea from there. However, like Mrs Goodman when she'd been with him, Moira wanted to walk along the front and also explore the pier.

'We'll have to pass The Floral,' Sam told her.

'Well, why not? We're not going into the place. After dinner, I insist we have a walk along the front. I don't want to sit in the hotel for the whole evening.'

'Fine. Fine.'

They enjoyed a delicious meal and after a leisurely drink, Moira said, 'Well, come on then, Sam.'

Reluctantly, he rose and accompanied his wife outside. A breeze was ruffling over the sea but it was a pleasantly warm evening. They strolled along arm in arm. They had never felt so close and happy in years. Sam was so grateful that Moira had forgiven him. Now he tried in every way he could to make up for his previous unfaithfulness.

'That's it over there.' He squeezed Moira's elbow. 'It's called The Floral because of the pots of flowers around it.'

Moira stared at it. 'Very pretty. I wouldn't think she'd want to ruin that place, if it's a good, money-making business, and I expect it is with that location. Oh look, is that a variety theatre on the pier?'

'Yes, but I don't think we'd get in to tonight's show without having booked in advance.'

'I could maybe spend an hour at the matinee tomorrow while you're doing your business with the warehouse people. I'll have a look around the town in the morning and then take in a show in the afternoon. It would be better than hanging around waiting for you in the hotel. I suppose you will be most of the day doing business?'

'Yes. In the morning certainly, and probably a good part of the afternoon. I'll get a ticket for you and we can arrange to meet afterwards. I could call for you at the theatre. We could have a meal somewhere. And I know a nice pub where we could have a drink afterwards.'

'That sounds fine. I'll look forward to tomorrow. If I find a nice little boutique in the morning, I might even treat myself to a new outfit.'

He laughed. 'I might have know there was a reason behind you wanting to visit South Castle-on-Sea. I can only be thankful that the girls aren't here as well. It would have cost me a fortune.'

They walked along the pier and he purchased a ticket. Then they walked further along the seafront until Moira said, 'I'm not used to all this exercise and fresh air. Do you mind if we turn back now, Sam?'

'No, of course not. Come on.'

Still arm in arm, they walked back to the hotel. That night, they made love with both passion and tenderness.

'Oh Moira, I'm so lucky to have you – especially after . . .'

She pressed her fingers against his lips. 'I don't want to hear any more about that. Not one word. It's in the past. We're both so much luckier than Mrs Goodman. We've still got each other.'

The next morning, after breakfast, he said, 'You know, you could have come with me, Moira.'

'What? Hang about in the background while you talk toys for hours? No thank you, darling. I'd rather do a tour of the boutiques. I'll see you later.'

They had arranged a time when they'd meet on the pier. He looked forward to being able to relax after his business meetings were over and to enjoying a meal and a few drinks with Moira.

Everything went according to plan until he returned to the pier. He found he was a bit early and he was standing gazing down at the sea when he heard a voice say, 'Couldn't keep away from me, could you?'

221

It was Viv. He turned to face her.

'Are you determined to end up in the jail? Because, if you don't get out of my sight right now, I'll report you.'

'Now, you don't mean that, darling.'

This was the real Viv. The weeping and apologising in court had just been an act.

'How many times must I tell you? Will you never be able to get it through your thick head? I don't want anything to do with you. I think you're mad. You tried to ruin my life. You ruined my home and everything I had. But you couldn't – and never will – ruin the thing that means most to me, Viv, and that is the love I have for my wife.'

Suddenly another voice cut in. 'And the love his wife has for him.'

'Moira, darling, I'm so sorry about this. I was just waiting . . .'

'You don't need to explain, Sam.' She turned to Viv. 'Now you heard what he said and, if he doesn't report you, I certainly will. You'll end up in jail, your business will be ruined. You'll be ruined. For God's sake, have a bit of sense, woman, and forget about Sam. You'll surely be able to find another man. A single man. You're not a bad-looking woman.'

Without another word, Viv turned away. She walked towards The Floral and disappeared inside.

Sam said, 'Good for you, darling. I must bring you down to South Castle-on-Sea more often.'

Moira linked her arm in his. 'I don't think she'll be bothering you again, Sam.'

He had a joyful feeling that Moira could be right.

'Certainly not if she thinks you'll always be here with me,' he laughed.

34

Miss Eden didn't know how Mr McKay managed to rent out his villa in Bishopbriggs. She always watched him as much as she could in the store, and she had a private arrangement with the security guard that he would report to her if he saw Mr McKay leaving. He had not reported any such sightings. Mr McKay could have left by the back door, of course. But he never used the back door except for the very occasional times he used that route to go to the bank.

However, she supposed he could have arranged the whole thing by phone with an estate agent. Anyway, as he eventually explained to her, he still had his mortgage payments to meet, plus other expenses connected with the house like the Council Tax. (And of course, although he didn't mention it, there was the money he was giving to her for his board and lodgings.) It was understandable that he would want to rent out his house. It had just been a surprise, that was all. No, more than that. How long, she wondered, were his tenants to be there? Had they a contract for a certain length of time, or what? She didn't like to press Mr McKay on that point in case he thought he had become unwelcome, and she was trying to get rid of him. He had been with her for a considerable time now and he seemed his old self again. Indeed, he seemed very content and happy.

They had long since got into the regular habit of sharing all the work in her flat. They even went together to do the food shopping and had lunch together during the week in the Marks & Spencer's café. They had their main meal in the flat in the evening. They shared the preparation and the cooking. On Sundays, they even went out for the Sunday newspapers together and made it the occasion for a little walk to get 'a breath of fresh air'. Often, they went in the afternoon and had a walk around Springburn Park. Sometimes they sat on a park bench and read the papers.

It was surprising how much they found to talk about – what had happened in the store, and what the staff were like, and what they were getting up to. They also had discussions and exchanged opinions about what was in the newspapers.

She was getting a bit worried that they were spending too much time with each other. He was definitely, to all appearances, perfectly all right now. One day, she suggested he should go out for the papers while she did something in the house. He agreed and went out, but as if he knew exactly what she would do, he turned and waved cheerily up at the window. She had not been able to resist the temptation to peep out to see if he was all right. He was safely back in no time, with the papers tucked under his arm. She had just got into the habit of worrying about him, she supposed. She had always treated any job she took on with great concentration, loyalty and seriousness. Nowadays, though, they laughed quite a lot, sometimes about what happened in the shop, sometimes at some comedy programme on television.

Now he went out regularly for the Sunday papers while she got the breakfast started. They heard that Mrs Goodman was writting a book, of all things. They both found that highly amusing, especially when Mrs Webster, who worked a couple of afternoons a week in Books and Stationery, told Miss Eden what it was about. It started her and Mr McKay remembering some of the poems and jingles of their childhood. They had quite a few laughs over that.

One day recently, she had seen him leaving the shop and she had discreetly followed him. Her heart sank as she saw him making his way along Argyle Street. He surely wasn't going along to see the group of tramps he'd once known? No, surely not. It was such a long time ago now. Then he had gone into a florist's, an Interflora place, and she realised he must be ordering flowers to be sent to someone. She wondered who the lucky person was.

First thing on her birthday morning, however, before she set off for work, a beautiful bouquet of flowers was delivered to her. Attached was a card which said simply, 'Happy Birthday, Miss Eden, from Mr McKay.'

She was quite touched at his thoughtfulness and that he had even remembered the date of her birthday. She never normally bothered about flowers but they certainly made the flat look cheerful and pretty.

That evening, Mr McKay insisted that he took her out for a birthday dinner. He had already booked a table at Café Gandolfi. It was really a most enjoyable evening. The food was excellent and the surroundings most interesting, with carved wood furniture and stained glass windows.

After the meal, Mr McKay splashed out on a taxi back to the flat. Altogether, it had been one of the best, if not *the* best birthday she'd ever had.

Eventually, she was tempted to say to Mr McKay that he didn't need to accompany her to her karate class any more. It must have become an awful chore to him. He had been going regularly twice a week for ages now. Then a thought occurred to her. He did look as if he was quite interested. Perhaps he would like to join. The physical exercise would be good for him. He really didn't get enough exercise. None at all, except for walking about the store and going shopping. The next time, on the way home from the karate meeting, she said to him, 'You've been coming along to the classes for so long now, Mr McKay. Why don't you join?'

He laughed. 'For goodness' sake, Miss Eden. A man of my age? Away with you!'

'No, I mean it. Age doesn't matter. Anyway, you're in your prime.'

He pushed his glasses further up his nose. 'I'm even short-sighted.'

'That doesn't matter either. Even if you never get to black belt standard, think of the advantages. It would give you a focus and targets. It would help you get the old heart and lungs fired up, basically stretch you physically and mentally . . .'

Mr McKay shook his head. He looked uncertain, but good-humoured. Miss Eden went on, 'It's all done in stages, teaching you how to stand, breathe, balance, and move. Come on, Mr McKay, try it, please. Just for me. *Please!*'

That made it a done deal. Next time, there he was, sheepishly shuffling from a chilly bare foot to a chilly bare foot, decked out in jogging trousers and a big, baggy T-shirt. He looked both nervous and embarrassed. Before long, the class was called to order and he was sent away from where he was standing with Miss Eden to the far end of the back row. There a young black belt in his twenties came to stand beside him.

'No worries,' he said. 'Just do your best to copy me through the warm up. If you're puffed or can't do anything, don't worry. It'll be a gradual process. Everyone has their own pace.'

The class was called to attention, backs straight, heels together, toes pointed out at a forty-five-degree angle, hands smartly by their sides.

On the command to bow, they knelt – left knee first, then right – and sat back on their heels. Then, as one, they leant forward – left hand first, then right, head briefly touching the floor, before they sprang to their feet. The bow he could manage with ease; the springing to the feet bit was more of a challenge.

Then it was straight into a sequence of bounces and bending and stretching that certainly gave his cheeks an unaccustomed glow. Slightly out of breath and most definitely warmed up, he was taken aside with two other newcomers by a slightly older black belt for the more tricky learning process, as individual techniques were broken down and explained.

He told Miss Eden later on their way home, 'Much to my surprise, I found the whole process both challenging and fascinating.'

'Oh good. And you'll enjoy it even more once you begin to master some of the techniques.'

'I would never have thought of joining the club. Thank you for suggesting it, Miss Eden.'

They bought fish suppers on the way home as a celebration and savoured eating them straight from their wrappings with their fingers.

'No use dirtying dishes at this time of night,' Miss Eden said.

It was unlike her to do or say such a thing. Completely out of character for both of them. It was just an unusual, out of character kind of night. However, they both meticulously washed their hands afterwards and gave their usual polite goodnights before retiring.

After a few classes, Miss Eden said, 'You are a quick learner, Mr McKay. You are getting really good at the karate.'

'Well, I enjoy the exercise. I feel so much more positive. I should have done something like this years ago.'

'Oh, I think you've always been positive, Mr McKay. After all, you've always been a good store manager.'

'More confident too,' he said as if he hadn't heard her.

'Well, karate certainly improves self-confidence, but I wouldn't have thought you needed your self-confidence built up. I mean, not now. It was your physical health and strength I was thinking of when I suggested you join the club.'

'Yes, I do feel physically stronger too. You'll have noticed that even my appetite has improved.'

She laughed.

'Yes, I think I'll have to put up your rent or you'll be eating me out of house and home.'

'Yes, I'm not paying nearly enough, Miss Eden.'

'Och, I was just joking. Of course you're paying enough. More than enough.'

Sometimes they did a bit of karate practice at home. He would ask about a technique and she would explain it to him and demonstrate it.

Then one evening, just as he was going off to his room, he turned at the kitchen door and said, 'I saw an advert in this morning's *Herald* about dancing lessons. All kinds – ballroom, even salsa. I was thinking, how about us attending classes for that, Doris?'

For a minute, she was so shocked at the unexpected use of her first name, she couldn't speak. Nor could she bring herself to reply using his first name. No way could she utter the word 'Norman'. But eventually, she did manage to say, 'Yes, I think I'd enjoy attending classes for that.'

'Fine,' he said and went away, smiling, to his room.

35

'Now are you sure you're going to be all right on your own, Mum?' John asked.

'Yes, of course, dear. I'm fine now.' She wasn't, but she could not expect John to stay with her any longer.

She waved him off with a smile on her face but fear in her heart. She made a determined attempt to quell the fear. At least the worst of the conflict with Douglas Benson was over. John had been with her when she'd told Benson about her move. His anger would continue to simmer, of course, and he would not give up trying to get rid of her from the store. But at least the first explosion of incredulity and rage had subsided.

Now here she was on her own and, as John had said, starting a new life. She didn't feel she was starting a new life. She looked out of the big corner window of the sitting room. From one side, she could see people relaxing *al fresco* at the tables of one of the cafés. They were sipping coffee and eating cakes. From the other side, she could look down at busy Ingram Street. From the windows of the kitchen and the bedrooms, the view was of the inner courtyard and designer shops. Here, Glaswegians could wander through the emporia of Armani and Versace. The setting was a combination of Victorian façades and the sculptor Alexander Stoddart's neoclassical statues with ultra-modern chic. There were Stoddart's bronzes of Mercury and Italia sitting on top of the wall heads. There were also Shona Kinloch's 'Wee dug' and 'Wee man'. The 'Wee man' was a budding Romeo throwing a kiss to his imaginary sweetheart. There was also a small greenery and water feature in the middle of the courtyard. As John said, 'What could be a more attractive and interesting place to live in the centre of a city?'

The flat itself was attractive, with its high ceilings and beautifully decorative cornicing. It had a dining room, as well as a fair-sized kitchen, with the latest modern fitments. She had no complaints about the flat or its situation. Except that it wasn't 'home'. It wasn't Huntershill. Tom had never been here.

The sitting room was not nearly as large as the one at Huntershill, and neither were any of the other rooms. Mr Webster had said that the sitting-room suite, indeed most of the furniture from the house, would not fit in, and would make the flat look crowded. There would hardly be any space to move around it. He had persuaded her to sell it and buy a new smaller settee and two easy chairs, and a few other pieces of furniture. Mrs Webster had gone to Goodmans with her to get the new furniture. Mrs Webster was very enthusiastic about some of the things they looked at. At the time, they had pretended everything was for Mrs Webster, of course, in case Douglas Benson should find out sooner than they meant him to. They wanted to make sure Abi was properly settled in and everything was completed first.

Abi just went along with everything that Mrs Webster suggested. Admittedly, Mrs Webster had excellent taste. In the end, it turned out the old curtains didn't match the new suite and so they had to be replaced too. There was nothing left of Tom any more. Nothing he had touched, nothing that had been handed down through the generations.

John had been carried along by the Websters' enthusiasm.

'Right enough, Mum. It's time you let go of the past. The Websters are right. The old house was too isolated for you on your own. And far too big. This new place will be the making of you. You'll soon be back to normal again. This is your new start in life. It'll do you the world of good. It's such a cheery, interesting place compared with where you were before.'

Where she had been before was with Tom. She tried to pass the time by looking out of the windows when she was in the flat. She couldn't pass any time writing the book. John had taken it away with him, so eager was he to try it out with Scottish publishers. She hoped he would not be too disappointed when it was rejected, as she was sure it would be. She didn't care.

John had taken Tom's office chair away from his office in the store. He desperately needed a chair like that for his desk in the flat on the Royal Mile, he said. 'You don't mind, do you, Mum? It would be just perfect for my desk. You don't seem to be able to buy chairs like that nowadays.'

She could not deny John anything and on this occasion, what would be the excuse? But oh, it was the last straw. Not even in her office could she look across and remember Tom sitting in that chair any more. And all the time, more than ever now, she could feel Douglas Benson insidiously undermining her. The strength to fight him was seeping away. So this was what it was like to grow older? No energy, no capacity to meet challenges. At one time, she had enjoyed a challenge. Anything new and challenging in life had even felt like fun. She used to laugh. She never laughed now.

Now, she just slumped back in one of the strange armchairs and tried to seek comfort in the familiarity of her *CSI: Miami* DVDs. Horatio was still the same. He was still tall and loose-limbed. He still stood with his jacket open and his thumbs hooked in his trouser belt. He still wore his shades. And, when he peeled them off, his eyes softened and narrowed with concentrated tenderness and understanding.

Every morning Abi walked along to the store and tried to keep her usual routine. She had her managerial meetings. She noticed, and was glad to see, that Mr McKay was looking well. He had suffered terribly when his wife died and his suffering had been stamped on his face for all to see.

She did her usual round of the departments and had a few words with some of the staff. Everything and everyone seemed to be ticking over normally. There were no problems or complaints. Of course, she paid all the staff well and there were plenty of good perks. She would have worked late but there was no excuse to do so. There was no putting off the time when she had to return to the flat.

Once she went out to Huntershill for a secret look at the dear old place. To her shock and horror, it no longer looked like her old home at all. All the trees and bushes had completely disappeared. At the side of the house was a glittering glass conservatory and a large patio of garish coloured tiles. There was garden furniture of glass and metal. A glass table had a tall metal thing that looked like a silver lamp sticking up through the middle of it. The beautifully carved oak door at the front of the house had been replaced by a white painted door, over which hung a red and white striped awning.

Her beautiful home had gone. She could never come back here any more, not even to look at the place. Once she got back to the flat, she wept brokenheartedly. She had to take a sleeping tablet to knock her out and banish the awful place from her mind's eye.

It still haunted her the next day. She could not get over it. Although she had left it, somehow she had always believed it would still be there, the same as ever. That day at the shop, Miss Eden had said, 'Are you keeping all right, Mrs Goodman? You look rather pale.'

'I didn't have a very good sleep last night. I get like that sometimes. I have a bout of sleeplessness. I must take a sleeping tablet tonight.'

'Well, I hope you'll feel better tomorrow.'

'I'm sure I will. But thank you for your concern, Miss Eden.'

Miss Eden had sharp eyes. She was an excellent detective. She missed nothing. Abi felt lucky in having her as an employee. It helped to know that, with such good employees, the store could keep running smoothly and successfully. Thinking of good employees made her remember Mr Webster. He'd been back down to South Castle-on-Sea and had experienced no more problems with the woman from The Floral. This was a great relief to both him and Mrs Webster, but apparently Mrs Webster occasionally went down with him for company. They seemed a very devoted and happy couple. She envied them.

Then something surprised her. John phoned to say that the book had been accepted by the very first publisher he had offered it to. He didn't just say the words in a normal manner, of course. Being John he was almost hysterical with joy and enthusiasm. He shouted so loudly, she had to hold the phone away from her ear.

'Mum, your book's going to be published. It's been accepted by the very first publisher I gave it to. I told you, didn't I? I told you.'

She shook her head at the phone. 'What on earth would anybody want to make a book of all that nonsense for, John? And who on earth would want to spend good money on it and read it?'

'The publishers know their business, Mum. They must know it will sell, otherwise they wouldn't have taken it on. Now you must come through and speak to them. I'll come with you to their office. It's not far from my flat.'

She felt a bit confused, partly because John was shouting so loudly. But a time was arranged for her to go and meet the publishers.

'They're going to bring it out very soon, Mum. It's just in time for their summer list, apparently. And there will be a launch party and everything. It seems the firm was about to go bust but it was saved by that guy I told you about.'

'Yes, you said he was eccentric and he must be, right enough,' she said, 'to fling his money about like that.'

'Och, it happens all the time, Mum. Taking over different businesses, expanding them, and so on.'

Oh yes, like what Douglas Benson wanted to do. There were too many Douglas Bensons in the world – in the business world at least.

Abi felt harassed more than excited when she travelled to Edinburgh for the meeting with Mr Thomas, the publisher. It turned out to be pleasant and businesslike. John was still simmering with excitement but the elderly man behind the desk in the office was quietly spoken and, after they discussed and then signed the contract, he took them out to lunch.

A launch party was arranged and at John's suggestion, it was to take place in the courtyard of the Italian Centre.

'There would be no room in the book department in the store,' John explained to Mr Thomas. 'With all the counters and shelves and show cases. But there's such a beautiful big courtyard in the Italian Centre. We could have a great party there.'

And so it was arranged. John enthusiastically offered to help. So did the Websters. Even Douglas Benson seemed pleased, as well as astonished. 'Now there's something new to concentrate on. There's a whole new career for you. A writer, who would have thought of that?'

'I did.' John laughed. 'I had quite a job persuading her but I managed it.'

'Good for you,' Benson said. Then to her, 'Well, well, so now you're a writer.'

She didn't bother replying. It was so ridiculous. The arrangements for the launch, however, kept everyone, including herself, very busy. Mr Thomas did not come to Glasgow to see what they were doing but his young woman assistant did, and reported back to him.

John persuaded Abi not only to purchase a new outfit for the event and have her blonde hair cut and styled, but to have a special facial as well. And on the big day, he cried out, 'You look wonderful, Mum!'

John had always been the same. He allowed his enthusiasm to completely carry him away.

Official invitations from the publisher had been sent out but members of the public could also join the party and hopefully buy a book. That, apparently, was the whole purpose of the event. Fortunately it turned out to be a beautiful, sunny day.

Abi sat at a table in the bright sunlight with a pile of books at her elbow which she signed as people queued up in front of her. The girl from the publisher's stood at the side of the table, ready to keep passing more books for her to sign.

At one point, Abi said, 'Is the publisher not coming?'

'Not Mr Thomas. But see over there – that's the guy who saved the company. I'll introduce you when he comes over. He's going to take you to dinner afterwards.'

There he was, tall and loose-limbed. He stood with his jacket open, his thumbs hooked in his trouser belt. He peeled off his shades, and his eyes narrowed and glimmered and his mouth betrayed a quirky humour.

She smiled. Suddenly, she felt the excitement of youth again and the mischief.

She winked at him. Then she went on signing the books.

Now her new life really had begun.